HALBMAN STEALS HOME

a novel

B. Glen Rotchin

DUNDURN

TORONTO

Editor: Shannon Whibbs
Design: Courtney Horner
Printer: Webcom

Library and Archives Canada Cataloguing in Publication

Rotchin, Glen
        Halbman steals home / B. Glen Rotchin.

Issued also in electronic formats.
ISBN 978-1-4597-0127-4

        I. Title.

PS8585.O84343H35 2012   C813'.6   C2011-903846-3

1   2   3   4   5   16   15   14   13   12

We acknowledge the support of the **Canada Council for the Arts** and the **Ontario Arts Council** for our publishing program. We also acknowledge the financial support of the **Government of Canada** through the **Canada Book Fund** and **Livres Canada Books**, and the **Government of Ontario** through the **Ontario Book Publishing Tax Credit** and the **Ontario Media Development Corporation**.

Care has been taken to trace the ownership of copyright material used in this book. The author and the publisher welcome any information enabling them to rectify any references or credits in subsequent editions.

                                                            J. Kirk Howard, President

Printed and bound in Canada.
www.dundurn.com

Dundurn	Gazelle Book Services Limited	Dundurn
3 Church Street, Suite 500	White Cross Mills	2250 Military Road
Toronto, Ontario, Canada	High Town, Lancaster, England	Tonawanda, NY
M5E 1M2	LA1 4XS	U.S.A. 14150

Halbman Steals Home

For my father

What is home then, you might wonder? The place you first see daylight, or the place you choose for yourself? Or is it the someplace you just can't keep from going back to, though the air there's grown less breathable, the future's over, where they really don't want you back, and where you once left on a breeze without a rearward glance?

— Richard Ford, *The Lay of the Land*

one

Mort Halbman couldn't explain why he was doing it again.

His body jerked forward then backward, forward and backward, as he braked and accelerated between the stop signs on Van Horne.

Damned stops. He'd always hated them, lined up along the short blocks west of Decarie until the stoplight at Clanranald, and then the one at MacDonald Avenue. How often had he sped through those yellows in quick succession to publicly demonstrate his disgust for the idiotic city-planners and legislators who'd put them there? Maybe the cops had nabbed him a handful of times over the years. The fines he'd paid were worth the pleasure of blowing through those yellows. And anyway, the money he'd saved in wear and tear on brake pads and discs had probably more than compensated for the cost of the fines.

Out of the corner of his eye, Mort mentally noted the spot where the street name changed from Van Horne to Fleet and the City of Montreal magically transformed into the Town of Hampstead. The squat, drab, brown and grey, Second World

War–era, attached, multi-tenant brick buildings morphed into two- and three-storey individual family dwellings on large lots that could barely contain them. In some cases, the houses sprawled over double lots with pools surrounded by spacious decks fenced in at the rear.

Mort felt his sagging shoulders rise slightly, his neck begin to tense up, and his fists tighten on the Jag's steering wheel.

He was going back. Revisiting the house he'd built almost thirty-five years earlier; before the Halbman-Solomon Cold War, before the BestTex Affair, before the flood, before the divorce, before the sale, before the fire.

In truth, you could hardly call 92 Hampstead Road a house anymore. What remained of it wasn't much more than a skeletal ruin. The walls were still standing, but the roof was gone, collapsed into the centre. All that remained of the vaulted living-room ceiling was a bare A-frame. Somehow, the twenty-foot-high panes of glass facing the street that were the house's most prominent feature remained intact, even if they were now tinted dark grey by a thick residue of smoke.

Mort had been returning almost on a daily basis for the past two weeks, as if the house, in its current blackened and devastated condition, had gained significance from the fire. It was like an ancient rock monument, a primeval shrine that mystically called to Mort, insisting that he visit regularly.

He'd succeeded for the past ten years to put the place more or less out of his mind. During that time he hardly ever drove into Hampstead at all. There was no need to after the divorce from Mona, or to be more precise, after the weekday morning he'd stayed home from work and quietly packed a valise — five business suits with ties to match, two pairs of cotton pants, five collared T-shirts, and his ever-growing assortment of toiletries and pill bottles — and left the house for good. It had been an orderly departure from an orderly life. No fighting. No hysterics. The date and time of departure carefully planned in advance and on schedule. Mona had made sure to be out of the house that morning. The kids were in school.

Whenever there were times he unavoidably had to be in Hampstead for any reason, to visit friends for example, he took detours so as not to pass by 92. But these days it was different. Mort couldn't help himself from coming back to see the house. He made special trips. It was beautiful again. Something about the way the remnant of 92 stood out from the surrounding neighborhood imbued the structure with a certain grace, a symbol of defiance. It instantly brought Mort back thirty-five years, to the day when the house was brand-spanking new, the first on a barren open lot of a section of Hampstead that had yet to be developed. In those days the old Hampstead Golf Club was still in operation on the other side of Fleet, and from 92 there was a clear view across the fairways and flag-dotted greens to the Hippodrome racetrack, and next to that, the huge shining globe of the Orange Julep on Decarie Boulevard.

Returning to 92 was not simply a case of nostalgia. The burned-out structure now possessed an otherworldly quality. It radiated a stark, grey, ghostly presence in contrast to the robust, earthy, overflowing flowerbeds and manicured lawns of the houses that surrounded it. Mort was irresistibly compelled to stand before the ruin of 92, to face it, and eventually step within the boundary of its scorched ground. It was, Mort imagined, how a person who appreciated fine art might feel in the presence of a painting or sculpture at a museum, though it must be said that he had never cared for art.

Mort drove past the Hampstead Park mound on his left and sped up around the curve before slamming on his brakes again, this time at the red light at the intersection of Queen Mary and Fleet. *This place doesn't let you build up to a head of steam*, he thought. The Jag's motor vibrated between his fists on the steering wheel as he waited for the green. His swelled right ankle began to ache from repeated braking and accelerating.

Notwithstanding the undeniably smooth ride, his luxury model vehicle had ceased being a source of pleasure and pride some time ago.

Mort made the illegal turn left from Fleet onto Minden Road. He slowed down and nodded to each door that he passed, roll-calling in his mind the names of his former neighbours: Shostak, Weitz, Hart, Mandelbaum, Fournier. He paused and repeated — Fournier.

What was Fournier's first name? He couldn't think of it. Mandelbaum's was Bernie, Hart's was Harvey, Weitz's was Abe, Shostak's was Murray, but Fournier?

Mort knew what each of his neighbours did for a living. Mandelbaum was an accountant, Hart was in retail, Weitz in construction, and Shostak, like Mort, was in the clothing business. But what did Fournier do?

And what was the crazy sonofabitch Frenchman thinking anyway when he built his house in Hampstead in the mid-1970s? It was a foolhardy act. Akin to Mort Halbman, a Jew, deciding to plant himself and his family down in the middle of Chinatown between the Wongs and Chens, or between the Bouchards and Lemieuxs in the east-end districts of the city where the virulent separatists draped blue-and-white fleur-de-lys flags over their balconies. Obviously, Fournier wasn't a separatist. Or if he was, he kept it private. He was most probably some sort of professional, a doctor, a dentist, or engineer who, like the Jews, habitually voted Liberal.

Mort vividly remembered the heavy equipment arriving to begin construction on Fournier's house. In those days new construction was a weekly event. Like everyone else in the neighbourhood, he'd figured the bulldozers and steam shovels had come to break soil for another Jewish family. The name of any new neighbour was typically known in advance, before the ink was dry on land transfer documents. Jews used only so many different notaries and word was passed quickly through the informal networks of the community: the golf clubs (Cedarbrook, Hillsdale, Elm Ridge) and restaurants (Snowdon Deli, Pumpernick's, Ruby Foo's, The Brown Derby).

But about this new family moving to Minden there was a discomfiting silence. A whispering curiosity slowly spread through the neighborhood and gradually amplified to anxiety-level over the three months of construction. They weren't Jews. This much everyone already surmised. There were rumours about blacks and Indians. An Asian family had bought property around the block on Glenmore and they typically drew uncles, aunts, and cousins from overseas. Could this be another Asian family? And if so, how many more were on the way?

If they were Asians at least they had taste. The elegantly-designed large brown bungalow fit in nicely with the bourgeois surroundings. The house had a stylish, curly wrought-iron railing and carved stone steps leading up to thick, dark brown, wooden front doors decorated with faux-gold floral trimmings. This touch allayed certain fears about the new owners.

One day a bottle of French red wine arrived with a card attached, reading: "Compliments of the Fournier family, your new neighbour at 7 Minden." Not counting the occasional distant wave and awkward exchange of faint smiles when Mort and Mr. Fournier found themselves watering their lawns at the same hour on humid mid-summer evenings, the gift and card would represent the only time Mort would have direct contact with his neighbour in over a decade of living virtually side by side.

What did Fournier think he was doing by moving into a Jewish neighborhood? Mort already knew the answer to that. The Frenchman was betting that the Jews would measure themselves against their neighbours, the houses would naturally get bigger, Cadillacs, Lincoln Continentals, and Mercedes-Benzes would multiply in driveways, and swimming pools would appear in backyards. He must have known that property values would soar. And they did. Smart Frenchman.

In the end, the Fourniers fit in. They were quiet, respectful, and kept up their property.

As he cruised past the brown bungalow with the faux-gold floral trimming on the door, Mort experienced an unexpected pang of guilt tinged with a certain sadness for not knowing Mr. Fournier's first name, or how he earned his living, and, truth be told, for never having extended to him a proper welcome to the neighbourhood.

Mort's Jag rolled past the house behind 92 belonging to the Flesskys: Bernice and Hy. He was a lawyer. She was a substitute teacher at the Jewish People's School, a job Bernice took to keep busy while her kids were in school. Mort wondered if the Flesskys were still living there. He wondered if any of his old neighbours had stayed. The Weitzs and Shostaks, he knew, had moved downtown to half-million-dollar, two-bedroom condos on Wood Avenue. Probably the others had abandoned Hampstead Road, too, after their kids, having graduated *summa cum laude* from universities in Toronto, Vancouver, or Boston decided their prospects were brighter if they stayed where they were.

The basketball net at 92 was still on the driveway, as solidly upright as the summer day in 1978 when Mort and Jackie had planted it in the ground.

Mort remembered that like it was yesterday. He could visualize a less paunchy version of himself standing over his hunched son, staring down into a hole while Jackie, sweaty from the heat and covered in a layer of grey dirt, dug hesitantly. Mort repeatedly urged Jackie to keep digging, deeper, and deeper. He wanted a thick foundation for the aluminum post. Mort was thinking about the upcoming winter and didn't want to worry about the post getting blown over in a blizzard once the heavy backboard and net were affixed on top. Jackie raised his head up periodically to protest, but dutifully obeyed his father and kept digging.

Father and son centred the aluminum pole in the hole, then Jackie mixed a bag of cement with water from the garden hose and poured it in. The next day the cement was solid and the new basketball net stood unsupported and erect.

Jackie was anxious to test it out. He couldn't wait to take the inaugural shot on Hampstead Road's first driveway basketball court. He made the rounds on the telephone, excitedly calling his friends to announce that the net was ready and to organize a pick-up game of three on three. In twenty minutes, five of his buddies were waiting on the driveway, ready to get the game underway.

His leather Converse high-tops laced, Jackie grabbed his brand-new official Kareem Abdul-Jabbar signature, NBA-approved Spalding basketball and headed outside onto the dark grey asphalt, his father trailing close behind. Mort wanted to be near his son when he made the first basket. A clean swish on the first shot, or even a bank shot off the backboard would bode well for the future of the Halbman family driveway basketball court.

As he approached the circle of kids gathered under the new net, Jackie immediately saw that something was off. He stopped short of the driveway and, ball still in hand — he didn't want anyone to take a shot while he wasn't looking — dashed back inside the house. In a few minutes he re-emerged with a rickety, paint-spotted wooden ladder hooked over his right shoulder, and gripping a measuring tape in his left fist. Jackie split the wobbly ladder open and threw it down directly under the basket. Without pausing to ask a friend to hold the ladder steady, he made his way up to the top taking two steps at a time, his face getting redder with each step.

The measuring tape was unspooled from the rim of the basket down, an inch at a time, until it touched the ground. He read what it said: nine feet four inches. The Halbman basketball net was eight inches short of the regulation height of ten feet. Jackie climbed slowly down the ladder and headed straight for Mort, who by now comprehended exactly what was happening.

Jackie stared at his father.

Then he said only one word in a voice loud enough for his friends watching on the sidelines to hear clearly.

"Loser."

It would be the only time Mort smacked his son across the face with the back of his hand.

Mort turned the corner from Minden onto Hampstead and stopped the car in front of 92. He waited there with the engine idling as if expecting something to happen. His ankle throbbed. Mort negotiated with himself. Should he leave the car and risk stumbling on a bum foot, or would it be wiser to stay within the confines of his vehicle and survey the ruins from the street? He decided on the latter.

What remained of the house was still an impressive sight. It was one of a kind. The only home in the whole Town of Hampstead, perhaps even all of Montreal, built completely out of stone — not a single brick. Mort felt his chest swell slightly with pride. The house was a monument to his industriousness and refusal to take no for an answer.

The year was 1969; the Summer of Love, Woodstock, and major league baseball coming to Canada with the Montreal Expos. The blueprints for Mort's new home were finally completed, but there was a hitch. The general contractor informed him that it would be impossible to build his home entirely out of stone within the allotted budget. The quantity of rock required was simply unavailable, and even if it were found, the transportation would be prohibitively expensive. Brick would have to be substituted. Mort refused to be discouraged. In a few hours he'd come up with a simple yet ingenious solution. The University of Montreal was blasting sections out of Mount-Royal to build a new sports complex. He would call them to ask if he could have some of the debris from their excavations. Realizing it meant saving on the cost of removing the heavy stone, they were more than happy to oblige his request. Imagine the stunned look on his contractor's face as hunks of beautiful Mount-Royal limestone arrived by the truckload. Ninety-two Hampstead Road was literally pieced together, stone by stone, out of the very heart of the city.

Through his car window, Mort could peer inside the indestructible outer shell of 92. There were piles of rubble and ash where the living room, the kitchen, and his former bedroom on the ground floor used to be. The innards were little more than a salvage operation. The only question was whether anything worth saving would be uncovered by digging through the charred debris. One way or another it would be a messy job.

Mort shifted the Jag into reverse and backed up slowly to get a better look at the bedroom side of the house facing Minden, when sudden honk-blasts from a BMW sports coupe screeching round the corner sent Mort's sore foot slamming on the brakes. The driver, a twenty-something kid wearing a freshly minted Montreal Expos baseball cap, gave Mort the middle finger as he swerved past. The gesture came with words.

"Old fuck!"

It may have been "Old fart!" Mort wasn't entirely sure. He was lip-reading.

"Oh yeah … oh yeah …" Mort yelled full-voiced as the car sped off. "Fuck … yourself.… And what would you know about it anyway? I was *there*.… Fucking punk.… I was *there!*"

What Mort meant was that he'd been *there*, on opening day, April 14, 1969, at Jarry Park for the very first Expos home game. He'd sat shoulder to shoulder with almost thirty thousand other delirious Montrealers to witness an 8–7 come-from-behind hometown victory over the St. Louis Cardinals, thanks to a three-run homer by Expo Mack Jones.

Mort had been *there*. He knew about years of loyalty to the ball club, about the ups and downs, about the joy and heartbreak. And there was plenty of joy. Just three days after the home opener, *Nos Amours* made history when Bill Stoneman pitched a no-hitter against the Philadelphia Phillies at Jarry, the first team ever to achieve that milestone in such a short amount of time.

Mort had been *there*. He'd attended almost every home game that first season. He'd even travelled to a dozen away games in Philadelphia, New York, St. Louis, and as far away as Chicago. It didn't matter that the Expos ended up in last place in their division with a record of 52 wins and 110 losses. He'd been *there*, seen it firsthand, cheered and jeered, but never gave up hope, not for a minute.

The baseball cap worn by the BMW punk was wrong. The colours were totally off. Lately Mort had been seeing that sort of sacrilege on the streets of Montreal more and more often. The Expos logo was popping up on hip-hop baseball caps, rhinestoned jean vests, and fluorescent pink and green bandanas. He lamented in his heart how, ever since the team had been sold to Washington and the name changed, the people who still owned the logo had been trying to squeeze every last penny out of it, devaluing and abusing it in the process.

Mort knew that certain things could not be sold. The *real* logo remained. It always would, in his heart. The odd-looking, fat, stylized, cursive, red, white, and blue insignia still meant so much. It was different from the structured, historical *B* worn by the Boston Red Sox, and the Detroit Tigers' stately *D*. It had nothing in common with the Philadelphia Phillies' streetwise, slanted *P*.

No, the Expos insignia was as incomprehensible and amorphous as Montreal herself. It was an *M* (for Montreal) and an *EB* (for Expos Baseball.) And if you looked at it in a certain way, the rumour was that you could see the initials of team founder and owner Charles Bronfman, the Jewish booze magnate.

But to Expos fans like Mort, none of those things mattered. The logo was not merely about the name of a team, or a city, or a billionaire owner. The logo was a thick-lipped, tri-coloured kiss on the forehead. It was childhood and a mother's love. It was summertime and sunshine and baseball, but not just anywhere. It was baseball in Canada. The major leagues in Canada. It was playing in the major leagues. And more importantly, it was *being* major league.

Mort was getting carried away again, losing himself in memory associations that popped up out of nowhere; a swearing punk swerving around the corner wearing a fake Expos cap, and opening day, and game-winning home runs, and all the seasons of hope and disappointment, childhood and mother-love. Mort was rarely ready for the flood of thoughts and feelings when they came.

Looking out his car window at what was left of 92, Mort found himself thinking that memory was the most important thing in the whole world because of all that it contained; not just past events, but meanings and emotions, too, the way a flowing river contained its own unique life, with vegetation and fish and a trillion unseen micro-organisms. When all was said and done, nothing mattered more than memories. They were all that a person truly possessed and the only thing nobody could touch. The house was gone but Mort still had his memories of it, and in this one sense at least, 92 would remain his forever.

The experience of drifting off in memory was new to Mort and it happened almost every time he visited 92. It was probably why he kept coming back. He enjoyed quietly slipping away into his private thoughts and feelings when no one was noticing.

This particular day, however, someone was noticing.

Mort lowered the driver side window as the man in uniform approached the Jag.

"Can I help you?"

Mort looked up, smiling quizzically. "I think the real question is whether I can help *you*." Mort didn't intend his reply to sound smart-alecky. He was feeling perfectly comfortable, in his element as it were, and the uniformed man standing in the middle of Hampstead Road with his hands on his hips, looked to Mort, decidedly out of place.

Mort sized him up; a large fellow, perhaps six feet, clad in dark blue poly-cotton slacks and a short-sleeve cotton shirt that was a lighter shade of the same blue. He had a full head of short, black curls, and hyphenating the centre of his rosy-cheeked, clean-shaven face was a thick, black, well-groomed mustache that reminded Mort of the one worn by comedian Avery Schreiber during his Burns and Schreiber days on the TV show *Rowan & Martin's Laugh-In*.

Mort instantly surmised that he wasn't Jewish. Italian, he guessed before it was confirmed by the laminated name affixed over the man's breast pocket: Potente.

"… Officer Potent."

"It's pronounced Potent*ay*."

"So sorry, Officer Potent*ay*. What I meant to say, Officer Potent*ay*," — Mort was enjoying repeating the name. Jewish people didn't have such virile names. They had nerdy, mushy appellations like Finklestein and Mintzberg. It was no wonder so many Jew-steins and Jew-bergs dropped the first part and became the more masculine Berg or Stein — "is that you have to be careful on the mean streets of Hampstead." He joked mildly. "Standing as you are in the middle of the road — you might get clipped by a Jewish kid in daddy's BMW blasting hip-hop music and blowing stop signs."

Mort's sightline drifted behind the officer as he spoke. He saw a maroon-coloured van parked across the street from 92.

"I saw what happened, sir."

"You saw what happened? What? And no sirens, no screeching tires, no giving chase, or calls for backup, or whatever it is that you guys do to catch dangerous hoodlums?"

"I'm not that kind of police officer. I don't hand out traffic tickets. I'm with Special Investigations."

"I see." And Mort did see, specifically the words CITY OF MONTREAL POLICE DEPARTMENT, SPECIAL INVESTIGATIONS UNIT printed across the side of the van.

"May I ask you a question, Officer Potente?"

"Certainly."

"Your first name. What is it?"

"Massimo."

"Massimo Potente. If you don't mind my saying so, your parents really knew how to name you. Massimo Potente. Sounds Roman. Massimo. Could be the name of an emperor. I bet there was an Emperor Massimo and he was the kind of ruler who could wake up on the wrong side of the bed and decide to send a dozen slaves to the lions. I tell you, Officer Massimo Potente, where I come from we weren't given names like that." Mort smiled demurely as he spoke, not wanting the officer to feel insulted. "May I hazard a guess and say that you were raised in east-end Montreal?"

"Saint Leonard."

"Just as I suspected. And if you don't mind one more question, Officer Massimo Potente, what did the kids in your neighbourhood call you? You know, your nickname?"

"They called me Mo."

"No kidding. How about that? I was named after an uncle Moe. My grandfather's brother, Moe Halbman. His Jewish name was officially Moses, *Moyshe* in Yiddish, but everyone called him Moe. They anglicized it and called me Morton. Morton Halbman. But everyone calls me Mort."

"Good to meet you, Mr. Halbman. Now, if you don't mind me asking you a question or two ..."

"Not at all."

"Any reason why you keep coming back here? It's not the first time I've seen you."

Suddenly, Mort felt a wave of unease wash over him. On the other occasions he'd visited 92 he couldn't recall ever seeing the maroon truck parked on the street. He'd seen various uniformed officials surveying the site in the immediate aftermath of the fire. There'd been police and fire department officials, representatives of the municipality of Hampstead, salvage workers, and no doubt insurance investigators, too. It was likely that Officer Potente was among them, though Mort wouldn't have remembered him specifically.

"Well, officer, I built this house, back in 1969. What a year, but you're probably too young to remember it. Woodstock, the Summer of Love."

"But you didn't own the house at the time of the incident?"

"No, sir. My wife sold it a few years ago. I lost the house in our divorce settlement. She got a good price for it, too. Almost ten times what it cost me to build."

"But this doesn't explain the number of times you've returned." Potente's tone wasn't accusatory, but Mort was increasingly feeling uneasy.

"I guess I've come back a few times because I'm feeling bad about what happened."

Mort instantly regretted making this statement. Except for the fact that his ex-wife had scored a bundle on the house he'd sweated to build and pay for, he had nothing to *feel bad* about, and using those words sounded incriminating. He was beginning to clue in to the fire investigator's line of questioning. He'd seen enough movies and TV shows to know how arsonists acted. Unlike other criminals, say murderers, arsonists tended to return to the scenes of their crimes. Firebugs had a unique pathology. After setting their fire they'd blend in to become part of the crowd, another innocent bystander who'd stopped to see what the excitement was all about: the fire trucks arriving, lights swirling, sirens blaring, the choreography of firefighters dashing about in their rubber suits, helmets, masks, oxygen tanks, and gear, carrying axes and hoisting ladders, unrolling hoses and hooking them up to nearby hydrants. The arsonist loved the spectacle of destruction, the consuming flames and great plumes of smoke rising into the air like a many-tentacled beast of his creation. And once the main event was over, the flames doused, and all that was left was a wet, charred, smoldering heap of wreckage, the arsonist would return for days afterward and be aroused by lingering visions and smells.

Mort's uneasiness in the presence of Officer Potente increased. He was under suspicion and being questioned.

"Not 'bad.' It's not that I *feel bad* about what happened. What I meant to say was that it's *sad* to see such a beautiful house destroyed. I mean I did build it, after all. I lived in it for seventeen years and raised two kids there. I'm sure you can appreciate that I find it very *sad* that it's gone."

"Of course, I understand. Did you have any relationship with the current owners, Mr. and Mrs. Shine?"

"No, never met them." Mort wasn't actually sure whether he'd ever met them or not. The Jewish community being so small and tightly knit, it was altogether possible, even likely, that he'd been introduced to the Shines somewhere, at Elm Ridge, or at a wedding or bar mitzvah. Under the circumstances, he felt it best to disassociate himself from them completely.

"Mr. Halbman, you don't mind if we kept in touch, do you?"

"That's fine."

"I may have one or two more questions to ask."

"I understand. Anything I can do to help."

Potente handed Mort a business card. "In the meantime, if you think of something that might help the investigation along, I'd be pleased to hear from you."

"Sure. Do you suspect foul play?"

"Well, Mr. Halbman, you may not have heard, but since it's in the public record, I don't mind telling you. The Shines had recently accepted an offer on the house. It was, in effect, between owners."

Mort raised an eyebrow. "There was no real estate broker's sign. Nothing to indicate that it was for sale."

"It was a private sale. Very hush-hush. An unsolicited offer had come in which the Shines had accepted. The closing was supposed to take place in a month."

"Who was the purchaser?"

"It's best if we speak again later, Mr. Halbman. Thank you for your time. Have a good day. And please, drive carefully!"

Mort nodded mutely. He watched Officer Potente turn and begin to walk away. Suddenly the arson investigator stopped, straddled the broken centerline of Hampstead Road, and smiled at Mort, who was still looking out through the Jag's driver side window.

"Oh, and by the way. You're right. It was a very beautiful house. I've seen pictures."

two

Mona's voice sounded crisp and self-assured on Mort's answering machine when he returned home to his one-bedroom apartment on the twelfth floor of the upscale *Le Cartier*, at the corner of Peel and Sherbrooke.

"Mort, there's something we need to discuss. Please call me as soon as you can."

No *Hello Mort. How are you? I know it's been a while.*

At some midpoint during what would become the last stage of their doomed marriage Mona had started taking on a new air of self-confidence. During marriage counselling — they'd gone for about six months in the seventh year of their union — she had adopted a new vocabulary and started calling her transformation "personal growth." Mort had heard about the so-called seven-year itch, but he preferred to think of that period as Mona's baseball-style seventh-inning stretch.

"I've changed," she'd say to him when she was annoyed at something Mort had done or said. It was almost always something he'd been *doing* and *saying* from day one of their relationship. "And you've stayed the same."

There wasn't a specific point during their marriage when Mort could say with any certainty that he understood what was happening to Mona *while* it was happening to her. She'd always seemed happy enough. There were no obvious signs of discontent. The house was kept clean. She made dinner every night and fussed over Jackie and Rusty as a good mother should. She was a dutiful wife. Not particularly enthusiastic in bed, but she'd eventually succumb to Mort's advances, satisfy his needs, and didn't expect much in return. If she was sexually unsatisfied, she didn't show it. Mort assumed that Mona was like most women, not as sexually eager as men were.

As best he could reckon *post facto*, Mort traced the beginning of the end of their mutual co-existence — in retrospect, he rarely thought of what they'd endured together for sixteen years as a *marriage* — to the expanding library of paperbacks Mona was reading and amassing throughout the 1970s and '80s. Titles like *How to Get the Love You Want*, *Healing Your Marriage, Healing Yourself*, and *Why He Wants to Control You*. Mona was a voracious reader, always had been. She consumed two or three books a week. At first they were mostly historical novels and biographies. But by the late 1970s, when self-help books had started climbing to the top of bestseller lists, Mona's need for them became insatiable.

Mort initially didn't mind the weekend projects of constructing new bookshelves in the basement to accommodate Mona's burgeoning collection. Eventually, though, the supply of books outstripped his motivation to play the weekend carpenter and books ended up on the floor of his workshop in stacks three and four feet high. The piles took the place of first, a new workbench with built-in vise grips, and then a deluxe rotary table-saw Mort had been eyeing for months in the Canadian Tire catalogue. There were hundreds of self-help volumes and when he entered the room he had to carefully navigate around the little towers. Mort cursed the cover of each volume as he crouched down to restack them when he inadvertently knocked a pile over. Titles like *Passages* and *More Passages* and *Next Passages*, which was ironic given that these books made it increasingly difficult for Mort to navigate safe passage across his workshop.

"Can't you give the books away after you've finished reading them?" he'd beg Mona. "Is it necessary to keep every single one?"

"Yes," she'd respond emphatically. "They're my reference."

Exactly what *reference* meant, Mort couldn't say, although, there was one moment of clarity during the divorce proceedings. In the course of enumerating Mort's failings, he expected Mona's lawyer, a well-dressed portly fellow with a thick salt-and-pepper moustache, to produce in court (with a surprise flourish *à la* Perry Mason) the most damning evidence against him: definitive expert opinions photocopied straight out of those books, which characterized Mort as the type of man who was an ample provider in a monetary sense, but uncommunicative, emotionally repressed, neglectful, and psychically damaged. And then the lawyer would pronounce the ominous-sounding diagnosis that Mort was borderline manic-depressive, obsessive-compulsive, narcissistic, neurotic, and abusive, meaning that he was a shitty father, husband, and person.

The resentment Mort felt toward Mona for impinging on his workshop space became increasingly difficult for him to bear. He needed that place. It was the one and only space in the house he had built solely for himself. The workshop was like his inner sanctum. It had taken him several years to plan, design, and set up properly. There were tools that he had purchased over time with great forethought: an electric drill; a series of saws featuring various lengths of blades for both wood and metal; hammers of all sorts; screwdrivers with a variety of heads, chisels, planes, and such. All of the tools had been organized and mounted on the wall according to size and purpose, woodworking tools on one side, metal and cement on the other. Along one wall he had cleared a workspace with a bench that had a heavy-duty vise affixed to the top where he could straighten nails and shorten screws with a hacksaw. He would spend hours there, engaged in the soul-purifying activities of measuring, hammering, and drilling. This labour was, Mort could now admit, his own form of self-help.

The unmistakable tone of certainty in Mona's voice on his answering machine could be traced back to her self-help books. It was a voice she owed to all the reading, all the so-called "personal growth"; stages of development in Mona's life for which Mort had paid a considerable price, and not just the cover price of all those books.

Although he didn't relish listening to Mona's tone — which, on second hearing, veered toward condescension — Mort played the recording three times to be sure of the words before erasing the message. "Something we need to *discuss*," is what Mona had said. What could possibly be left between them that needed discussion?

Mort surmised that it must concern Jackie since Rusty called regularly to check up on him. Jackie remained tight with Mona, even if he rarely contacted his father anymore.

"Hello."

Mort was relieved that it was Mona's voice on the answering side and not that insufferable Gordon's.

"So what's the big emergency?" This was Mort's way of dissing Mona for not asking "How are you?" on his machine.

"Thanks for returning my call so quickly."

If Mort had known that Mona had left the message not long ago he might have waited longer to call back.

"No problem. So?"

"I'm fine, thanks, and how are you?"

"Okay. I suppose you've already heard about the house. I was over there today," Mort said flatly.

"Yeah. Shocking."

"Yup."

"You know Mort, in spite of everything, when I heard that 92 had burned down, I felt horrible."

"Really, Mona? I would have thought that you'd get a good chuckle out of it. Maybe have a little dinner party with your literary friends to celebrate. After all, you got out when the going was good and cashed in. It was some other family's life that went up in smoke."

"That's cruel, Mort."

Mort never forgave Mona for being awarded the house in their divorce. She'd lived in it for five years and then when the kids were old enough and, coincidentally, the real-estate market was at its peak, sold it for three times the value accorded it in their settlement. The way she profited had burned Mort.

"It was an electrical fire? Is that what I read in the paper?" Mona said.

"They don't know yet. There's an investigation."

"You mean they suspect arson?"

"Maybe, I don't know. Look, I don't have all day. Why'd you call?"

"Well, I was talking to Jacob this morning."

Mona had never called their son Jackie as Mort did. Jacob Hillel Halbman was the name that appeared on his birth certificate, after Mona's maternal grandfather. But to Mort he'd always be Jackie, after Jackie Robinson who'd spent one glorious season in Montreal playing ball for the minor league Royals before heading out to Brooklyn to make sports history by breaking the colour barrier.

"How is Jackie?" Mort asked. There was no doubt that Mona — having read about this sort of thing in one of her books — considered Mort's insistence on calling their son Jackie something he did merely to undermine her. At least Mort hoped so.

"Great, actually."

"Good."

"And that's what he wanted to tell you ... himself, actually ... in person, but asked me to speak to you first."

"What did he want to tell me himself?"

"That he's doing great."

"Then he should have called me."

"Mort, listen. Remember when Rachel started going to Torah classes and you weren't thrilled about it?"

"Okay."

"And remember when she started lighting Shabbat candles and going to synagogue and you weren't too pleased about that, either?"

"Okay."

"And remember how mad you were when the rabbi fixed her up with an orthodox boy from his community —"

"Mendel." What kind of parents would make a boy go through life with a name like Mendel? As kids growing up on Fairmount Avenue, Mort and his friends used to tease Mendels. Yankels and Yossels, too. *Mendel, Mendel kak in fendl!* — they'd sing — *Mendel, Mendel, shits in a pot!* And this Mendel's last name was Fuchs. A double curse!

"Things didn't work out so bad, did they? Rachel is happy. She's a great mother ..."

"You know, Mona, it only took one generation for the kids I grew up with named Fuchs to change it to Fox. And what does my daughter do? She goes backwards. She Yiddishizes her name from Rachel to *Rochl*, calls herself *Roochehleh*, for godsakes! *Roochehleh Fucks*."

"It *is* her name. And you know as well as I do that it was necessary to help Rachel fit in with that community, *her* community."

To Mort, Rachel would always be Rusty. It had been obvious from the very first moment he laid eyes on her in the hospital. She had emerged from her mother's belly nine pounds and two ounces with a full head of strawberry-blonde hair, her skin rosy as fresh fruit. If Jacob would be Mort's homage to the great Jackie Robinson, then he could not let a difference in sex stand in the way of christening Rachel May Halbman in honour of the great Expos slugger and right fielder, Rusty Staub, a.k.a. *Le Grand Orange*.

"Look, Mona, get to the point. Are we talking about Rusty or Jackie here?"

"Like I said, Jacob is doing great, he's very happy, because he's found someone special. And he wants you to know."

"I could have heard that news from him."

"And he's getting married."

"He's what?"

"You'll like his partner. Very smart and successful. In the financial services business like Jacob."

For a very brief moment, when Mona said *partner*, Mort thought of a girl.

"When did *this* happen?" Mort muttered.

"When did *what* happen?"

"You know … how long have you known?"

"About Jacob having a boyfriend?" Mona suddenly sounded incredulous.

"About him wanting —" Mort could barely get the syllables out for lack of breath, his chest tightening "— to get married?"

"He's been talking about it for a while."

"And you encouraged him?"

"Get with the times, Mort. Remember the wedding of the Melnick boy from around the corner on Gayton Road last year? Gordon and I were invited."

Mort remembered all right. When news got around he'd felt sick for poor Norm Melnick, a respected accountant in the community. In his prime, Norm had been a star athlete at the Y and the envy of every red-blooded Jewish male. He'd married Ruthie Plotnick, Fairmount High's Betty Grable, great legs and tits to match. A few years ago he'd won the club championship at Hillsdale.

"It was the social event of the season. At the Ritz-Carlton. His bride was a psychologist from California. I mean his *partner*, of course. They made such a handsome couple. They even filmed the whole thing and I don't mean for home video. For TV, a documentary on gay marriage in Canada. Mort, Jacob wants us to be *involved*."

Involved. Mort hated the sound of that word. People used it when referring to illicit sex, as in, "She got *involved* with him," or when denying criminal allegations, as in, "I wasn't *involved*." Mort definitely did not want to get *involved*.

"What do you mean by *involved*?"

"He's not asking you to pay for the wedding, if that's why you're sounding so concerned. He and his partner — his name is Noah, Noah Benaroch — have plenty of money. They're planning a beautiful affair. Jacob wants us to participate. You know, as his parents."

NOW APPEARING AS JACOB HALBMAN'S PARENTS IN THE PERFORMANCE OF HIS GAY WEDDING appeared in Mort's mind on a theatre-sized, light-bulb framed marquee.

"Don't tell me he's having a goddamned ceremony, Mona."

"In a synagogue. With a rabbi. Well, maybe not in a synagogue. Maybe at a hotel downtown. Anyway, they've already started calling around."

"You can't be serious?"

"They've looked into the Sheraton and the Delta."

"Please, stop."

His only son was a homo. This, Mort had already pretty well come to terms with. According to Mona who had read extensively on such things, Mort had successfully made it through all the psychological stages: Denial leading to Anger followed by Bargaining, then Depression, and culminating in Acceptance.

Jackie was sixteen when he sat his parents down in the living room on Hampstead Road, calmly looked into their eyes, smiled like he was about to announce that he'd just won first prize at the high-school science fair and said, "I love you both and I'm gay."

From that moment on and for months afterward, Mona made Mort's life a living hell. She took every opportunity to announce Mort's psychological stages as if they were Gay Pride Parade floats passing by one at a time.

"Don't worry Mort, it's natural to deny that you have a gay son. *Denial* is the first stage of trying to come to terms with loss." Then came, "It's perfectly normal to be angry Mort, and to be asking yourself, 'Why me?'" After that: "Soon you'll be bargaining, Mort, looking for ways to change Jacob, and when that fails you'll feel depressed. But it's all okay because those are the towns you have to pass through before you can arrive at the land of *Acceptance.*"

No kidding. That's exactly what Mona had said. *Those are the towns you have to pass through before you can arrive at the land of Acceptance.* It was a phrase that had stayed with Mort ever since, etched indelibly in his memory, seared with a branding iron on his brain.

Hearing those words — quoted straight from one of her books — the thought thundered through Mort's head that if Mona had her druthers she'd probably choose that line as the epitaph on his gravestone:

> *Morton Halbman*
> *1936– ?*
> *He passed through*
> *Denial, Anger, Bargaining and Depression*
> *on his way to Acceptance.*

So here he was, years later, and according to his psycho-babble-loving ex-wife, now a tax-paying resident of the land of

Acceptance. In Mort's mind, he'd planted himself in the county of *Anger*, bought a lot, built a house, and made friends with the neighbours there.

All of Mona's psychological mumbo-jumbo came back to haunt Mort years later (like he always knew it would) when he discovered that Jackie had started selling mortgages over the telephone. One of Mort's buddies had mentioned that he'd seen Jackie cruising around Hampstead in a brand-new Porsche convertible. Mort immediately called Mona to ask what was going on.

"He got a job," Mona said.

"A job? What kind of job?" *Drug dealer* was what flashed through Mort's mind.

"In financial services," Mona answered.

"Financial services? And, pray tell, what does 'financial services' mean?" *Financing drug deals*, Mort thought.

"Well, I'm not quite sure, but it has something to do with brokering mortgages."

"Brokering mortgages? How can Jackie broker mortgages? Did he take a course and get a licence? Does he work for a bank?"

"No, he does it over the phone."

"Over the phone? I've never heard of such a thing. How long has he been doing this?"

"About eight months."

"So he's been working for eight months, selling mortgages, and he can afford to buy a Porsche? Aren't you a little suspicious, Mona?"

"It's a very good business and growing fast. And Jackie's a very smart boy. I always knew he would be successful."

Mort made inquiries. Mona had been telling the truth. It was a loans business. In fact, a lot of young people were selling what they called "sub-prime mortgages" and making a killing. They were barely out of high school and in no time driving Mercedes-Benzes and BMW sports cars, showing up at the best restaurants, and drinking at the city's most exclusive nightclubs. Mortgage call centres were springing up all over the city. A hard worker and charmer over the phone, Jackie was a natural at it.

"People don't say no to free money," is what Jackie told Mort when his father phoned to ask him about it. "Well it's not exactly *free*, but the payments, at least for the first little while, are reasonable enough. And when they find out that I'm prepared to throw in an extra five or ten grand on the spot, they get *boners*.

"They usually need immediate cash to pay off credit card debt. Especially in California, that's where we focus our calls. They tend to be over-extended there. But then I toss in what I call *the bonus*. If I find out that they're driving a five-or six-year-old car I ask if they'd like to buy a new one. I tell them that by leveraging the value of their house, I can make it possible. Within twenty working days of receiving their signed agreement they can receive the cash in their account. Everyone's got dreams. I turn their dreams into reality. I'm a fucking fairy godmother."

"Sounds to me like you're turning dreams into nightmares," Mort said. "If you already know they're overextended and they're not likely to be able to make future mortgage payments, aren't you just helping them dig their own graves?"

"It's only sport," was Jackie's answer. "A big game. And I happen to be very good at it. Look, there's a ton of available cash out there. Lending institutions are itching to make loans and then sell them off as commercial paper. If I didn't take advantage of the situation, someone else would."

After initially feeling awful about how his son was earning a living, Mort found that it faded. He told himself that what Jackie was doing was, in fact, perfectly legal. And Jackie was right about one thing: someone else *would* come along and do it if he didn't. Pushing loans on people was just doing business. And it was a good business, too. Mort even started feeling pride, *naches*, when he learned that Jackie had made a down payment on the purchase of a condo without having to come to Papa for the money.

But then all the good feeling dissipated and was drowned out by Mona's irritating voice in the back of his mind repeating, *the first stage is Denial*. Mort began questioning: How had Jackie, who'd always been such a caring, sensitive boy, gotten himself messed up in that dirty business? Queers, as a rule, weren't like that, were they? When had queers become like all other regular blood-sucking schmucks?

And now, on top of everything, the gays wanted to get married; have a rabbi or priest sanctify their union before God. It was bad enough the parents had to be *involved*. Now they wanted God *involved*, too. Mort shook his head. The gays obviously had no idea what the hell they were getting into. Didn't they see that the rest of society wanted less to do with marriage? Couldn't they take a hint? The grass was always greener, Mort decided.

"When you say that Jackie wants us to be *involved*," Mort said to Mona, "what exactly does he want? That we should walk him down the aisle together? Give him away?"

"He thought we might start by meeting his future in-laws. He's made reservations for all of us at the El Morocco."

"Oh, hell."

"Mort, for godsakes, please try to give Jacob this chance. It may be too late for you but he deserves a shot at happiness."

"Oh, jeez."

three

"Y'know, sometimes Halbman, you're a prime number-one meshuganner."

Mort smiled. Coming from Gerstein, he knew it was meant as a compliment.

"I think you're getting nuttier in your old age."

Mickey Gerstein was one to talk. He knew something about meshuganners. Since the mid '70s he'd been traipsing around Hampstead, Côte Saint-Luc, and Snowdon wearing faded Levis, snakeskin cowboy boots, and a grey Stetson like he was the Jewish John Wayne. He'd never been able to let go of the "urban cowboy" style.

A tall man with a square jaw, Gerstein could almost still pull it off. These days, though, as his face took on the double-chinned roundness that came with age, his cowboy getup was beginning to look clownish. The silver horseshoe belt buckle he wore was almost completely covered by a thick, low-hanging gut. A little face paint and Gerstein's Stetson wouldn't be out of place among the maroon-tasselled fezs and miniature cars in a

Shriners' parade. He maintained a swagger, which he'd claimed was actually the remnant of a hip injury sustained in a skiing accident twenty years earlier. Since that time he'd carried an imitation ivory walking stick (he refused to call it a cane) with a handle carved into the head of a stallion. He didn't really need the walking stick anymore, he said, but kept it because it came in handy when he had to bash a street punk's head in, which, if you believed his stories, happened with a certain odd regularity.

The only thing missing from Gerstein's Jewish cowboy schtick was a Texan drawl, and there were certain moments — like when Gerstein looked up from his seat at the waitress and said, "I'll have a side order of kreplach with extra onions, darling" — that Mort could swear he detected a Southern twang.

Gerstein, the king of meshuganners, had now christened Mort one. Looking around the table, Mort realized they were all a bunch of meshuganners. After thirty-five years of meeting at the Snowdon Deli every Sunday morning and sitting in the same booth, they'd gone from being a bunch of up-and-comers, to gin players, to cigar smokers, to golfing buddies, to fishing partners, to their latest incarnation as a club of meshuganners, a gathering of *alta-cackers*, doddering old fools who compared colonoscopies and talked about whose doctor had the softest hands the way they used to discuss MVP infielders, Golden Gloves replaced by rubber gloves. It was lunacy. The years had left them this way. Or maybe they'd always been a little ridiculous, slightly laughable and off-centre, and it was only now becoming entirely apparent to everyone.

But through it all: the card games, golfing outings, fishing trips, the marriages and divorces, mistresses and remarriages, the kids and stepkids and eventually grandkids, through all the permutations and combinations, they'd always had each other, and until recently, they'd always had the Expos.

For twenty-five years, the Snowdon Deli gang had shared a block of box-seat tickets along the third base line, first at Jarry

Park, then at Olympic Stadium. Almost every Sunday morning in the summer, before going to the game that afternoon, they'd talked baseball, sized up the visiting team, analyzed the pitching duel, and assessed the home team's chances. For twenty-five years they'd had humdinger debates. Would Expos ace starter Steve Rogers win the Cy Young this year? Would outfielders Andre Dawson and Tim Raines, or first baseman Warren Cromartie capture the National League batting title? Incredibly, one year the team had had three players in contention. The Expos were in their heyday. Anything was possible. It was their turn to take a championship. That was the consensus among the Snowdon Deli boys and all Montrealers. That is, until October 19, 1981.

That day the Expos faced the Western Division champion Los Angeles Dodgers to see who would be heading to the World Series. With the best of five series tied at two games apiece, the rubber match turned out to be a classic pitcher's duel between Expos starter Ray Burris and Dodgers rookie sensation Fernando Valenzuela.

Tied 1–1 going into the ninth inning, and looking as if the game was headed for extra innings, Expos manager Jim Fanning made a fateful decision. He opted to bring in his ace starter Steve Rogers to pitch in relief of Burris.

"The most moronic move in the history of baseball," Gerstein said, later at the deli. "A career starter pitching in late-inning relief. It made absolutely no sense."

Mort defended Fanning's decision. "Rogers had stymied Los Angeles in game four. Fanning was going with his hot hand."

"Everyone knew Rogers was a slow starter. And he was pitching on only two days' rest," Gerstein countered. "His arm was overworked."

"Some slow starter," Mort said. "He dispensed with Garvey and Cey, the first two batters he faced, clutch hitters both, easily."

They debated around the table at the Snowdon Deli for weeks, guessing, second-guessing, and triple-guessing Fanning's decision to pitch Rogers. Once that issue was exhausted (unresolved), they moved on to pitch selection. With the game tied, two outs in the ninth inning, and no one on base, catcher Gary Carter called for the sinker against Dodgers centrefielder Rick Monday. Rogers nodded his agreement.

Should Rogers have dealt his sinker? Why not a safer, more reliable pitch? His fastball or curveball?

"The sinker was too risky to pitch on a three and one count and with a World Series appearance at stake. There was too much room for error," Mort argued. "Rogers could have gone straight at Monday with his fastball. Monday was strictly a contact hitter not a slugger, and not even in Cey's or Garvey's league."

"But that's exactly why Carter called for the sinker," Bookie Moss said. "The stats on Monday showed he wasn't a power hitter. In their wildest dreams they never imagined he was capable of slamming even a missed breaking ball out of the park. They took a chance."

"Yeah, but Monday was having a good day," Hershy Blank added. "He was responsible for the run that tied the game in the fifth inning."

"Exactly. Monday had punched a single to shallow right field in the fifth. So that's what they figured he was capable of doing if he made contact with a breaking ball in the late innings. Not hit a homer," Mort said.

The consensus was that Carter and Rogers could not have reasonably expected that a lifetime .264 hitter in the waning years of a respectable (not stellar) career was capable of smashing a missed sinker out of the park.

"A seasoned pro like Monday is always capable of hitting the right pitch for a homer," Gerstein cautioned.

Mort could still visualize every detail of that terrible moment: The lanky, mustachioed Expos ace leaning toward home plate to read the catcher's signs, straightening up, cupping ball and glove under his chin. Mort could still feel the anticipation in his bones, the calm before the wind-up, an interlude just long enough for a prayer to be silently uttered: *Lord, may the ball be protected on this dangerous journey and arrive at its destination, the catcher's mitt, unscathed.*

It may have been the cool, damp weather conditions that day, or Rogers's overworked arm, or simply a temporary loss of concentration, but the sinker delivered to Monday on that Monday was obvious and timid and utterly without guile. It hung up and crossed waist-high right over the middle of home plate.

Carter saw it coming. He'd seen it, as catchers can, from the moment the ball left the pitcher's hand, and even before then, in the wind-up. And so did Monday, like it was all happening in slow motion, and he swung with confidence, nice and easy.

Mort claims he saw it coming, too.

36,491 gasps: the number of fans who'd shivered through cold drizzle and stayed put for every rain-soaked inning because they were warm inside, heated by the flame kept close to their hearts of World Series hope. Each heard the crack of Monday's bat and simultaneously felt their heart break on the spot. Among the 36,491, sitting along the third baseline and helplessly watching the Rogers sinker sail over Andre Dawson's head (and the centre-field wall he'd guarded so acrobatically for 108 games), were Mort Halbman, Hershy Blank, Bookie Moss, and Mickey Gerstein.

Mort remembered how after Monday, October 19, 1981, "Blue Monday," as it would be forever known in Montreal, the Sunday morning discussions around the Snowdon Deli table would never be the same. Weeks of fruitless debate about Fanning's decision and Rogers's pitch selection were followed by renunciation. When Mort would raise the subject of the Expos' prospects for the upcoming season (it was invariably Mort who did), a pall would settle over the group, a pregnant silence that said, *zog nisht*, don't say it, remember what happened the last time the taste of victory was on our tongues. It faded to bitterness and we were left with nothing but hunger, an empty ache in the gut.

Mort didn't care. He ploughed on, steadfastly refusing to abandon the old baseball debates or ditch the old hope. There were years when the Expos fielded competitive teams. The analysts agreed that they had the best farm system in all of baseball, one that consistently produced future stars. It didn't matter that players like Pedro Martínez, Larry Walker, Moisés Alou, and Vladimir Guerrero, who'd been brought up by the Expos organization, would eventually find stardom, big salaries, and win championships playing for other franchises in U.S. cities.

For a while the boys debated whether a new stadium downtown would save baseball in Montreal. That argument was finally put to rest by the team's departure for Washington. From that point on, none of the boys, except Mort, wanted to hear another word about baseball. When the Expos left town, it was as if they'd taken the whole history of Major League Baseball in Montreal along with them. Montreal would revert to its natural state, a hockey town now and forever.

Mort, on the other hand, couldn't help from talking baseball. He'd accepted the moratorium on reminiscing about the Expos, but baseball as a general topic was not necessarily out of bounds. He was telling the boys about something he'd recently read in *Newsweek* on whether a batter was more likely to smack a curveball or a fastball out of the ballpark, when Gerstein, the Jewish John Wayne, had pronounced him a *meshuganner*.

Mort was saying that U.S. university researchers had proven conclusively and contrary to conventional wisdom that a curveball was more likely to be hit for a home run than a fastball. The scientific breakthrough had been made possible through recent advancements in technology enabling researchers to accurately measure something called Magnus Force, the spin of a pitched ball.

"So we've always thought that the faster a ball comes at the batter, the faster the batter has to swing and *zing-o*, the more likely it is that the ball clears the fence." Mort clapped his hands together for effect. "But actually, a fastball has backspin. So when the batter takes his cut, his swing reverses the direction of the spin when it makes contact with the bat."

"I don't know who's more of a meshuganner, you or the scientists and their universities who spend money on this shit," Gerstein said.

"No, seriously," Mort continued, "a curveball crosses the plate with topspin. So when the batter makes contact he's actually speeding up the spin, which increases the lift of the ball as it leaves the bat."

"What are you saying?" Hershy Blank suddenly piped in. "And what's it got to do with anything?"

"Yeah, cut the shit already, Mort," Gerstein said.

"What I'm saying is —" Mort paused to think "— what I'm saying is that when it comes to curveballs, it's not the speed of the bat that matters, it's about making contact. A nice and easy swing is all it takes to hit one out of the ballpark." Of course, he was thinking again, consciously or subconsciously, about the fateful day Rick Monday launched Steve Rogers's sinker out of the ballpark ending Montreal's hope for a championship. And probably everyone sitting around the table understood this, although no one dared to mention it openly.

It was at that very moment, as if he'd just made contact with something deep inside himself, that Mort's impeccable logic and passion for the game drained from his body. He paused to catch his breath.

Mort stared at the scoop of chopped liver and onions sitting like a baseball on the center of his plate and silently regretted what the baseball discussion had become. They no longer had a team to root for, so Mort hung on by talking about university studies. It was a pathetic display, akin to all the other discussions they'd been having lately at Snowdon Deli that centred on doctors and the latest scientific advancements in medicine. Where they used to talk about on-base percentages and batting averages they now discussed cholesterol and triglyceride numbers. Gerstein was right. Mort *did* sound cuckoo for bringing it up.

What a bunch of losers we are, Mort was thinking as he surveyed the faces around the table. Losers, not in the sense that they hadn't made successes of their lives, each had in his own way. Gerstein had made a fortune in wholesale furniture. Portly Bookie Moss with his light red hair and stylishly cropped grey beard had made a good living importing musical instruments and electronics. Sleepy-eyed Hershy Blank had made money in the scrap business. But Blank's real payoff came when the municipality decided that the land he owned along the Lachine Canal was too valuable for a scrap yard and expropriated it. He'd been retired for over twenty years and still drove a Lexus.

When Mort thought about his buddies being a bunch of losers he hadn't intended it in a derogatory way. What went through his mind was that each had lost a son or a daughter to another city, Toronto, Vancouver, Calgary, somewhere in the States, and lately to Hong Kong or Shanghai. Like the Expos players who'd skipped off to better teams in more lucrative markets, the next generation of the Snowdon Deli gang had moved on to places where career pastures were greener.

Mort's kids had stayed in Montreal, but in a way he'd lost them, too. Jackie now played for the queers and Rusty for the Lubavitchers. His losses were piling up. Put 92 Hampstead Road in that column, as well. It was increasingly looking like an unsalvageable season; prospects were grim. Were these the curveballs he was really talking about? Was he subconsciously referring to Jackie and Rusty when he spoke about Magnus Force and making solid contact with a nice and easy swing?

"My son's getting married," he heard himself blurt out to the table.

It was never easy to shut up the Snowdon Deli group. Now, there was stunned silence. Not even Gerstein spoke. They all knew that Mort had only one son and that he was a *feigele*. No one mentioned it out of respect for Mort. The subject had been taboo.

Finally Blank hesitantly broke the silence, uttering the question that was on everyone's mind.

"D'you mean ... to a woman?"

"No," Mort said.

Bookie asked, "He's getting married here? In Montreal?"

"I didn't think ..." Gerstein began.

"Yeah. It's legal these days. Marriage certificates, spousal benefits, the whole shebang," Mort interrupted.

"Even for Jews?" Gerstein said.

"Apparently."

"Nah, I doubt it. Not here, anyway. Not in Montreal," Gerstein said. "Maybe they can have a civil ceremony, get a judge to marry them. Those guys will marry anyone these days. But an official Jewish marriage between gays in Montreal? Nah. They'll never be able to find a rabbi in this city who'd do it."

"They say they've been interviewing."

"Interviewing? Interviewing who?"

"I don't know. I guess one of the lefty rabbis. Reform or Reconstructionist."

"There are only two synagogues like that out of eighty in the whole city."

"Maybe they're not looking at congregational rabbis. Maybe they're looking at a free agent. Or maybe they're planning to import somebody from out of town, from the U.S., for example, where they have a ton of Reform synagogues."

"Shit," Gerstein said, sounding defeated.

"Who are they inviting?" Blank asked.

"The usual. Friends, family."

"And you?" Bookie asked.

"Me, what?"

"Who are *you* inviting?"

Mort immediately understood Bookie's question. "Not you, if you don't want to be invited. Look, fellas, it's okay. Don't worry. It's not like I'd be offended or anything if you didn't want to come," Mort said, beginning to feel offended.

"I'm out," said Gerstein, who was Mort's oldest friend. "It's just that —" he paused, gathering his thoughts. Then the whole table watched as Gerstein bowed his head like he was about to say a blessing over the plate of kreplach in front of him. He calmly cupped the top of his Stetson in his palm and gently lifted it off his head. There, to Mort's astonishment, sat a skullcap the diameter of a softball.

"What the hell?" Mort exclaimed.

"Well, you remember when my mother died, the rabbi who did her eulogy? Nice man. He did such a good job. Anyway, we talked a few times after that. I made some donations. He's doing important work in the community. Helping kids with disabilities. Then he asked me to come for Shabbos lunch. After that it was a Torah class once a week."

Mort stared at Gerstein in disbelief. "You never mentioned it. I never thought *you* of all people...."

Gerstein shrugged. "Well, you know how these things can be sometimes. We wear many hats in life."

"Look at him." Mort turned to Hershy and Bookie.

"Your hat was always a baseball cap, Mort. So now mine's a kippah."

"Suddenly he's a philosopher," Mort scoffed. "Meshuganner."

four

Melvin Grand of the law firm Shalinsky, Grand, Poirier & Associates had been Mort's trusted legal counsel for more than thirty years. He'd seen Mort through more than one tight spot. It had taken a while, but Mort had finally forgiven Mel for screwing him over during the BestTex hearings by assigning a junior from the firm to plead his case. All of that was water under the bridge when Mort called Mel for his advice on what to make of his encounter with Officer Massimo Potente, which had annoyingly remained in the back of his mind for days.

"So what happened exactly?" Melvin asked.

"Well, I went over to 92 Hampstead Road for a look and he was there. A big strapping Italian from Special Investigations. At first everything was friendly. We chit-chatted about our names and he told me about how he grew up in Saint Leonard. Then, out of the blue, he started interrogating me."

"What do you mean by *interrogating?*"

"He started digging, asking probing questions in that sneaky detective sort of way you see on TV. It made me nervous."

"What did he ask?"

"He wanted to know why I had made repeated visits to the house over the last few weeks since the fire."

"And you told him —"

"I built that house. Why the hell shouldn't I visit to see what was left of it? And actually, have you been by to see for yourself?"

"Yes, I have."

"It's held up pretty good, eh? Wouldn't you say so?"

"It was a well-built house." Melvin had been involved. He'd helped Mort with all the legal matters that surrounded the purchase of the land, ensuring that all the necessary municipal permits were in place, and the builder's contract was in order.

"The structure is completely intact. All that beautiful Mount-Royal limestone. The house was between owners when it burned down. Did you know that?"

"Between owners? What do you mean?"

"The house was sold, but the sale wasn't completed."

"Impossible."

"Impossible? What's impossible?" Mort asked nervously.

"*Between owners* is impossible. The house can't be sold when the sale was not completed."

"But that's what I heard."

"It can't be what you heard."

"Goddammit, Mel, don't tell me what I did or did not hear. That's exactly what I heard."

"Okay, so whoever told you that it was between owners was an idiot."

"Actually, it was Officer Potente who told me."

"Okay, so Officer Potente knows fuck-all about the law if he said that."

"What's your point?" Mort asked, his frustration building.

"Officer Potente's an idiot."

"That's your point?"

"Yes."

"Look, Mel, I don't give a shit if Officer Potente is an idiot or a saint. I wasn't calling to talk about him."

"Okay, so?"

"The police suspect arson. And because I happened to be there a few times they think that I had something to do with it."

"Did you?"

"Did I what?"

"You know."

"Start the fire?"

There was a point in almost every conversation between them when Melvin Grand would start answering Mort in mono- and duo-syllables as if he had better things to do, more lucrative problems he'd rather be handling. This conversation had reached that point.

"How many years have we known each other, Mel?"

"A lot."

"And how many times have you screwed me over? Like during BestTex when your junior almost got me sent to jail! Remember that?"

"Okay, Mort, calm down."

"The putz advised me to co-operate with the commission, squeal like a pig, and rat on my own father-in-law! I could've killed you for sending him in your place. I swear, Mel, I don't know why I stayed with you all these years!"

"Okay, okay, Mort. I'm all yours. I'm listening."

"What I want to know is who actually owns a house in the interim period between an accepted offer and the date of closing?"

"Legally, the vendor is the owner of the house until the deed of sale is signed by both parties. That's why I said Officer Potente knows shit. There's no such thing as being *between owners*. It's either one owner or another."

"So, let's say there is a mishap, like a fire, between the accepted offer and the closing, and the house is destroyed. What happens? I mean there's no house to sell, right? So, who sustains the loss?"

"Theoretically, both parties. The vendor loses the house he owned, and the purchaser loses the house he wanted to buy. So you might say that it's a double-loss. But I know that's not what you're asking. In principle, it's the vendor's obligation to deliver the house in the same condition as it was at the time of the offer."

"And if he can't?"

"All bets are off."

"No deal?"

"Exactly. Assuming the fire was an act of God, of course, the vendor can walk. Although you can imagine a scenario in which the vendor and purchaser sit down together and hammer out a mutually agreeable arrangement to go through with the sale."

"How?"

"Simple. The purchaser pays the previously agreed-upon price, or a newly negotiated amount, and the vendor rebuilds."

"With the insurance money?"

"Yes."

"And if the fire wasn't an act of God?"

"A fire is usually considered an act of God, unless it's a blatant case of liability."

"Such as?"

"Such as someone getting drunk and falling asleep with a lit cigarette in his mouth."

"What about an electrical fire?"

"Typically considered an act of God."

"What happens when there's liability?"

"If liability is suspected, it has to be proven, and ha, ha, that's when things get *interesting!*"

Mort heard Melvin's voice raise one register. His lawyer was finally getting excited.

"Couldn't the buyer just accept the vendor's insurance settlement and decide to rebuild on his own?" Mort asked.

"It's possible," Melvin replied. "That would be up to the two parties to work out."

Mort finished the discussion feeling comforted. Perhaps the story of the house he'd built wasn't ending after all. Maybe, it was just beginning.

The next day, his conversation with Melvin Grand still rattling around in his brain, Mort risked another run-in with Officer Potente and returned to 92.

Driving down Minden Road toward Hampstead, he pressed his forehead against the Jag's windshield over the steering wheel. At the intersection, Mort peered around the corner to look for Potente's maroon van in front of the old Wolofsky house across from 92. Just in case it was there, he was getting ready to take a sharp left on Hampstead Road in the opposite direction. To his relief, the van wasn't there. Mort rolled to the right, easing his foot onto the brake in front of 92.

The property was encircled by a fence. Inside stood an idle Caterpillar backhoe looking as if it were a giant caged insect, its massive hydraulic shovel tucked like a claw against its body. The innards of the house were gone. The centre was being excavated. All that was left of the living room, kitchen, dining room, and bedroom were deep holes. Charred wooden joists and support beams stuck out from mounds of debris like charred bones of a partially devoured prey. The house's stone carapace, however, remained perfectly intact. Mort felt reassured.

Surveying the site, Mort could reconstruct all of the contents of the master bedroom in his mind's eye; the grey shag carpeting, the king-size bed with the leather-encased headboard, the ensuite bathroom covered in octagonal alternating black and white tiles with built-in shower, and the closet that ran almost the entire width of the room where he and Mona hung their respective wardrobes at opposite ends.

The closet had full-length sliding mirror doors. Countless mornings, Mort stood in front of those body-length mirrors wearing a pressed shirt, checkered boxers, and nylon socks, and knotted, unknotted, and re-knotted his imported silk tie, frustrated that he couldn't seem to get the length right. Then he would give up and just stand there staring at himself, dreading the start of another workday, the tie twisted and hanging awkwardly off his shoulder like a noose.

Running mirrored doors the entire length of the room was Mona's idea. Mort had never liked it. For one thing, the mirrors distracted from television-watching. After work, Mort's ritual was to kick back in his recliner with a glass of rye whisky on the rocks and watch the six o'clock news. Light from the TV would reflect off the mirror doors and bounce all over the room. It took Mort months to train himself to ignore the effect. Making matters worse, Mona insisted on several more mirrors in their bedroom, one above the bathroom vanity where she could apply her makeup, and another hanging next to her side of the bed at eye-level directly opposite the closet. When Mort stood in front of the closet doors he saw his reflection echoed backward in the mirror behind him like at a barbershop. He remembered how disconcerting it felt to see the back of his head being sucked into a deep, unending, curving tunnel of multiplying frames. Their bedroom was carnivalesque; more like a haunted house of mirrors than a tunnel of love.

Above the closet with the mirror doors there were cupboards where Mona kept the household papers, bills, bankbooks, investment certificates, and other documents in neatly labelled file folders. Mona was an organized person and Mort trusted her to take care of their important papers. Those cupboards were also where Mona had stashed the cash-filled envelopes from BestTex. And where Mort had kept Shimmy's briefcase after the scandal was over. It was a conspicuous location which, somehow, the provincial police had overlooked.

* * *

I'm fucked. I'm dead.

These were the first two thoughts that shot like two bullets through Mort's skull when Detective Raymond Lambert of the Quebec Provincial Police said, "Do you take me for some stupid Pepsi?" Lambert was smirking as he spoke, a boy-are-you-ever-screwed grin.

When Lucy came into his office announcing that Detective Lambert was back and wanted to see him, Mort didn't flinch. He couldn't even be bothered to lift his eyes up from *The Gazette* Wonderword he was working on at his desk. By now, months after the commission investigating corruption in the garment industry was launched, Mort was accustomed to being questioned by the authorities. What he didn't see coming was the search warrant. And Lucy had neglected to mention that the detective was accompanied by four other police officers.

Lucy had barely turned to leave Mort's office when Lambert blew through the door, brushing rudely against her. His four associates were already in the accounting office in front, rifling through filing cabinets as the warrant was dumped on Mort's desk. Mort kept his composure. He raised his head slowly and greeted his guest with a smile.

"Detective Lambert."

"Mr. Halbman. I have here a document that allows us to search the premises."

"Make yourself at home." Mort wanted to show that he was unfazed.

"You can expect that we will be here for some time. We will require your co-operation."

"Of course."

"In addition to the records of all your fabric purchases, invoices, packing slips, and sales journals, et cetera, we will require access to your patterns and markers."

Alarm bells sounded in Mort's head. He'd never heard an investigator refer to "markers" before. Needletrade lingo.

"Yes, sir," was all Mort could say.

"We've done our homework, Mr. Halbman."

"Homework? What do you mean?"

"Do you take me for some stupid Pepsi?"

"Excuse me?"

"We know that a skirt and a pant take approximately a half yard of fabric. A jacket about one yard."

The alarm bells in Mort's head subsided just long enough for him to hear that voice pronouncing self-judgment: *I'm fucked. I'm dead.*

"We now have the simple mathematical know-how required to verify that your fabric purchases, as reported, are justified." Detective Lambert's formal tone, the repressed gloating, was beginning to grate on Mort's nerves. Lambert sat down across the desk from Mort.

"We will simply tally up the yardage from your fabric purchases and compare this to the number and type of units you have reported in your sales journal. Then we will balance this against your markers and style numbers as well as your inventory. For your sake, Mr. Halbman, you better hope that everything matches up."

Mort remembered his initiation into the invoice-buying scheme. Shimmy Solomon had been pulling cash out of his business by buying phony fabric invoices for years. BestTex Fabrics was his and the industry's principal and most reliable purveyor.

Shortly after Mort married Mona he was summoned to his father-in-law's office. Shimmy's tone was casual, "Come up and see me, please, when you can." Mort understood that when Shimmy said, *when you can*, he really meant, *now*. Mort had never kept Mona's father waiting, anyhow. Like so many other manufacturers, he idolized him. Shimmy owned Simple Dress, the largest manufacturer of ladies' ready-to-wear in the country. When Mort was introduced to Shimmy's daughter, he could hardly believe his luck.

It was 1959 and Mort had been working for five years in his older brother Hymie's small dress company. One day, Shimmy's sister Dottie was in their showroom on Phillips Square. Dottie owned a small shop on the Main and bought dresses from Hymie. Mort entered the showroom just as Dottie was mentioning that her niece was "on the market." She was about Mort's age, a looker, and owned a red T-bird convertible. Normally, Mort would resist being fixed up. In this case, the car was enough to sell him on the blind date.

Less than a year later, in the presence of the bigwigs of the Montreal *schmatta* business in a lavish wedding ceremony at the Ritz-Carlton, Mort became Shimmy's son-in-law.

Mort never gave a thought to working for Shimmy. He knew that his father-in-law would have gladly taken him in to head up one of his many divisions. Mort always knew he would stick with Hymie who'd bailed him out after his Hollywood fiasco. From then on, Mort worked hard to prove his family loyalty, eventually earning his way to full partnership in Halbman Dress.

In theory, Mort and his father-in-law were competitors. In practice, no one competed with Shimmy. He was in a class all his own. On a personal level, Shimmy liked Mort and was happy to share trade secrets with him to ensure that his daughter would be well provided for. Shimmy talked about strategies for knocking off European styles and gave Mort tips on cost-cutting design and manufacturing techniques. Mort drank in the lessons, building Halbman Dress into a success.

So when Shimmy said, "Come up and see me," Mort didn't hesitate.

The ritual in Shimmy's office from that first meeting onward always remained the same. Shimmy kept a vinyl brown briefcase tucked in behind the two-tiered black metal filing cabinet in the back corner of his office. He'd roll his chair along the speckled grey carpet to the filing cabinet and extract the thin, rectangular briefcase by the handle from its hiding place. Then he'd roll back and lay it down flat on the desk. The cash was already inside. Shimmy would hand Mort the key to the safe-deposit box and blurt out a number. Twenty-five. Fifty. A hundred. One time the number was one hundred eighty. Mort would never forget that day. It would turn out to be the highest number he'd ever hear from Shimmy. One hundred eighty. Mort would also never forget the weight of the briefcase, his struggle to swing it back and forth trying to make it look light as he strolled casually into the bank. He remembered the feeling of being alone in the bank's restricted area where the safe-deposit boxes were, the anticipation of flicking open the gold latches, and the light that the briefcase would emit once it was open with one hundred and eighty thousand in cash staring up at him.

Once, in the street just outside the bank's door — the briefcase was filled with one hundred twenty thousand that day — Mort recalled patting the outside of his pocket. He did this regularly to verify the presence of the safe-deposit box key. He touched, patted, rubbed, grabbed, and dug frantically. There was no key. He backtracked, five paces, ten paces, fifteen, twenty, scanning the corners of the sidewalk where he had stepped, his eyes sweeping in front, the heat rising in his body, the sweat condensing on his brow. And then, by some miracle — how else to explain it — there it was, a gold glint in the light of the midday July sun winking at Mort less than an inch from the gutter and poised to tumble into it. In a fraction of a second the key was safely back in Mort's iron grip.

"Do we have to do this, Mr. Halbman?" Detective Lambert asked.

Mort didn't hear the question. He was preoccupied with trying to stop himself from sinking deeper into a pit of emotional quicksand.

"What?"

"Do we have to do this?"

"Do we have to do what?"

"This. The searching. The mess."

"Why are you asking me that? You have a warrant."

"Well, you can end it right now?" Lambert said, grinning again. "Surely you must know that it's not *you* we're really interested in."

"What?"

"I don't expect we'll find very much here, anyway."

Mort wasn't aware of it, but at the same time that Lambert's team was turning his office upside down there was a second rubber-gloved squad hungry for a search ringing the doorbell at 92 Hampstead Road.

"Mr. Halbman, Mrs. Halbman is on line one for you. Please pick up!" The secretary's voice split the air, wedging Mort's attention momentarily away from Detective Lambert. "Mr. Halbman, Mrs. Halbman says it's urgent. Please take line one."

"May I?" Mort stared at Lambert, who nodded.

Mona's voice was frantic.

"Look … calm down. Calm down … don't worry. Let them do what they want. It's fine … don't worry. They're here, too. I'll be home as fast as I can. Just let them do what they want, okay? Bye."

"It's finished, Mr. Halbman. This game. The smart player knows when to cash in his chips. We've already been to the offices of BestTex. We've seen his files and Halbman Dress appears frequently. Not to mention Simple Dress."

Mort couldn't pry his eyes off the telephone receiver replaced in its cradle.

"You must know that you can be helpful to our investigation. I will call my men off if you agree."

"Agree?"

"Yes, to co-operate with the investigation. Tell us what you know about your father-in-law's activities."

Years later, after his runs to the bank for Shimmy, after the investigators had done their work, even after Shimmy died, Mort kept the vinyl briefcase in the closet above the sliding mirror doors in his bedroom at 92. Now he wondered what had become of it. For all he knew, Mona had chucked it in the trash after the flood, along with the rest of the family keepsakes, heirlooms, photos, and souvenirs she had deemed "unsalvageable."

Mort remembered the times, before the divorce, when he would take the briefcase down and wipe the dust off the gold latches on top. There were no dents or scrapes on the briefcase, which always surprised him considering what it had been through, how many cash-filled trips it had made. Sitting on the corner of his bed, he'd prop the briefcase up on his lap and try the locks. They usually opened easily. The springs were tight and the hollow *thwack* of the mechanisms flipping open, first on the left, then on the right, always sounded good to him, a perpetual reminder of the years when the dress business thrived and the money flowed. Then Mort would reclose the locks, pressing the tiny golden arms down. This task made him struggle. The upper and lower halves of the briefcase never seemed to close squarely on its hinges, the latches didn't fit properly into their slots. Mort would check the edges to make sure that they were square. Then he'd try the locks two or three times until they finally clicked into place.

Mort had taken cash to Shimmy's safe-deposit box in that briefcase maybe two-dozen times in total, hundreds of thousands in cash, perhaps millions. He'd learned plenty from his father-in-law, including how to take tax-free money out of his own business by buying phony invoices, envelopes of cash he'd hand over to Mona, which she'd slip into her files in the compartment above the mirror doors of their bedroom closet.

Mort refused to co-operate with Detective Lambert and his investigation. He always was and would remain a loyal son-in-law. But he knew that to Shimmy he was less valuable as a son-in-law than as a bag man, a mule, someone to carry his briefcase for him.

Mort pled ignorance under oath at the commission hearings. He never regretted doing it, even as Mel Grand's junior was counselling him to tell the inquiry everything he knew, spill all the beans. What the hell did he know, that *pisher?* Had he listened, it would have gotten him into major-league trouble and probably would have helped send Shimmy to prison. He relied on his instinct under examination and denied everything. Shimmy avoided jail time (probably by bribing the right people, although Mort couldn't say for sure) and ended up paying a hefty fine, one he could comfortably afford. Lambert's men made their calculations and Mort ended up paying a fine, too. He may not have gotten the free pass he'd been offered, but Shimmy helped him to pay the bills, so he wasn't badly hurt. And who were the big winners? The lawyers, as usual. They took home more than the government did.

Mort returned home the evening that Lambert's men had ransacked both his office and home to hear Mona's description of how the cops had checked everywhere, turned over every drawer, and every closet and cupboard inside out, even in the kitchen.

"Well, *almost* every closet. Somehow they never checked the bedroom closet," Mona explained. "Except to admire themselves in the mirror."

five

There was nowhere else Mort would rather *not* be at the moment than in his car driving over to meet Mona and her insufferable boyfriend Gordon for dinner at the El Morocco restaurant. Check that. There was one place he would rather not be and that was actually sitting at the table trying to make conversation with them and the family of his gay son's boyfriend (or should that be fiancé?). This time spent in the Jag, he reckoned, was probably going to be the highlight of his evening. He popped a recording into the Jag's cassette player, Richard Harris singing "My Boy."

"My Boy" had been his favourite song when Jackie was still a kid. Mort hadn't been able to listen to it since the divorce. It was too painful hearing Harris achingly intone in his deep, fatherly baritone, *You're all I have my boy, you are my life, my pride, my joy, and if I stay, I stay because of you, my boy.* Mort hadn't stayed.

Mort had stumbled upon the recording in the back of his bedroom cupboard one afternoon. Having returned from another visit to 92, he'd decided on the spur of the moment to

clean out the closet, a chore he'd been avoiding for a long time
and not one he could rely on Charlene, his Filipina housekeeper,
to accomplish. He was feeling generous that day and he knew
that there were enough outmoded shirts, tight-in-the-waist
trousers, and threadbare, faded sweaters to fill a garbage bag for
the Salvation Army.

The sight of the "My Boy" cassette sitting at the bottom of a
long-ignored brown cardboard box startled him. It was nestled
among a half dozen 8-track tapes, three transistor radios, a tangle
of wires and A/C adapters, and a handful of old, crusty batteries.
He felt his heart sink when he recognized what it was. Sensations
were instantly dredged up; sitting by the living-room fireplace at
92 on Sunday afternoon, eyes closed, listening to the song's sad
swelling violins, the image of a regally-garbed Richard Harris
playing King Arthur in the film version of *Camelot* floating
through his head. The actor was aglow, bathed in stage-lighting,
which bestowed upon him an aura of self-possession, control,
and perfect authority. The picture never failed to make Mort feel
buoyant and temporarily at peace.

Mort dug into the cardboard box and brought the cassette
to the surface. He stared at the transparent rectangular case with
trepidation. It was scratched, but otherwise in good shape. He
felt simultaneously gripped and weakened by the object and
couldn't put it down even though a large part of him wanted to.
Would it sound the same after so many years? What new or old
feelings would it evoke?

Getting the cassette into the car was the first step to playing
it, but Mort was hesitant, and the recording would spend several
days in the Jag's glove compartment. On his drives over to 92
Mort sensed the tape's presence in the vehicle. After a while it
became intolerable. He knew that the only way he could break
the object's spell would be to muster the courage to play the
damn thing, which he finally did one day after speaking to Rusty
on the phone.

She'd made her weekly call to her father before sundown on Friday. As usual, there was no pretense. Mort knew that Rusty was calling because she religiously abided the Fifth Commandment to honour her parent. This was her *mitzvah*, her way of reassuring herself, in the lead-up to celebrating the Holy Sabbath, that she was indeed a good daughter. Mort didn't look a gift horse in the mouth. He appreciated the effort, regardless of her motive.

They exchanged "hellos" and "how was your weeks." Mort asked about the kids, the regular script was followed, interspersed with perfunctory chit-chat, although this time their rhythm was stilted. The casual silences that typically punctuated their dialogue — characteristic of a parent and adult child who have very little left in common — grew heavy and unsteady. Pauses accumulated between them like water filling a glass bowl to the rim. A spill was inevitable. Who was going to make the false move? It was Rusty.

"Mom called," she said.

"I figured. She called me, too."

"Yeah, she mentioned that you'd spoken. Dad ... I don't know what to say."

Father and daughter were on exactly the same page. Mort felt relieved.

"It's okay," Mort said.

"I mean 'mazel tov' doesn't seem right? You know?"

"Yeah. I know."

"Mom said Jacob was happy at least."

"Yeah, she told me the same thing. And *she* sounded ecstatic. Did she mention that they were planning a ceremony? That they were actually looking for a rabbi?"

"Yeah. She even asked me if I could suggest any, me being religious and all. Can you believe it? Boy, sometimes she's so clueless."

Mort smiled. He hadn't felt this close to his daughter in a long time.

"Did she mention anything about dinner at the El Morocco?" Mort was hoping that Rusty might have been invited, too. He'd have an ally at the table. It was possible that she and her husband could come. The El Morocco was a strictly kosher establishment.

"No."

"I guess it's just for the parents then."

Mort began thinking again about the choice of restaurant. He didn't go in for middle-Eastern cuisine. He was a Gibby's man, a Moishe's Steakhouse guy. He couldn't fathom how people survived without consuming an occasional blood-dripping rib steak or fried hunk of liver every once in a while. Meat was not supposed to be ground-up, spiced, and rolled into pastry shell. As for side dishes, he understood dill pickles and cole slaw, not hummus and tahina. Bread was meant to come sliced from a thick loaf of pumpernickel or rye, not circular and hollow like pita.

If Rusty and her husband weren't invited, then why was a kosher restaurant chosen? Mona and Gordon certainly weren't kosher. Mona knew zilch about being kosher. Milk and meat were not separated in her kitchen at 92. She'd been raised in a secular household and attended Iona School and then The Study, a rich kids' private all-girl school up the hill in Westmount. She hadn't had a smidgen of formal Jewish education. And the Solomon family traditions were anything but religious. On Friday nights they dined at the Garmento's eatery of choice, Ruby Foo's on Decarie Boulevard, where pork spare ribs, breaded Chicken Soo Guy, and the famous Poo-Poo Platter were feasted on. The only *Jewish* subjects Mona's father ever spoke about with enthusiasm around their home were Freud and Marx. Shimmy read books on them continuously. He related to their theories because both Freud and Marx shared a common worldview to which Shimmy also subscribed: that modern Western man and society were fundamentally ill. Shimmy believed it with every fibre of his being. "Society is sick! We're all sick!" He would declare as he paced back and forth across the living room of his Circle Road home, a thick book swinging in his hand like a brick about to be launched.

Watching her father pace, and hearing him pronounce on the inevitable demise of the capitalist system and the murderous Oedipal complex in the hearts of men, Mona soon grew to understand why, in spite of his wealth and prestige as a successful businessman, her father seemed distant and unhappy. It didn't surprise her one iota when only a few years after closing Simple Dress, the doctors at the Jewish General Hospital proclaimed that her father was dying of an inoperable, particularly virulent type of cancer. She did not shed a single tear — although she wanted to — less than a month after the diagnosis, when she stood beside Shimmy's hospital bed and witnessed his final breath. "Sick," was her only comment, whispered stoically to herself.

Being a witness to her father's tome-swinging tirades and fits of despair taught Mona about the power of books. It was a lesson that would stay with her forever. Her father had enjoyed books as a source of insight, pleasure, and comfort, and so would she. Mona absorbed another lesson about her father: that there was nothing he loved as intensely or unconditionally in his life as his books, including her mother and her.

If it wasn't for Mona's benefit that a kosher restaurant had been chosen for this little family get-together, Mort thought further, then it had to be for the other side of the marriage equation. What did Mona say was Jackie's boyfriend's name? Noam or Noah? And his last name was Ben something ... Benhaim ... Bendavid ... Benami ... Ben ... sonofabitch! It struck Mort like a stone against a car windshield. A mockie! Jackie was marrying a Moroccan. That explained the El Morocco. Not that Mort had anything against Moroccan Jews. It was just the way they had made their presence so conspicuously felt in the Jewish community lately. On his visits to 92, Mort passed brand new three-storey Moroccan-built monstrosities with triple garages and pools where houses built by his former neighbours used to stand. All over Côte Saint-Luc and Hampstead the Moroccans were bashing down homes and erecting bigger ones that stuck out and interrupted the neighborhood flow. They had every right to build whatever they wanted, of course. It was just that their homes were utterly devoid of character and taste as far as Mort was concerned.

Their synagogues were conspicuous, too, sprouting up all over town. Not that Moroccans were any more observant than other Jews. But as a generation closer to immigration they were excessively reverent of tradition and superstition. They continued practices that Mort deemed primitive. Even completely assimilated Moroccans kissed doorposts on their way in and out of rooms.

Mort had never had many personal dealings with Moroccan Jews, either in business or socially, but these days it was practically unavoidable. Bad enough that his son was getting hitched to another man, it was to another breed, a Sephardi, a mockie, it was a mixed marriage! If he'd had a speck of hope for the couple to begin with (he didn't), it was absolutely gone now.

When he spoke with Rusty, Mort didn't pry into her feelings on gay marriage. He didn't have to, knowing full well that it was categorically contrary to her religious beliefs. Still, he had a dozen questions that he would have liked to ask, starting with if there was any chance she would ever consider attending a gay marriage ceremony, and whether she would make an exception for the marriage of a close family member. Hell, Mort wasn't sure about the answers to those questions himself. He decided not to bring it up with Rusty. Better not to agitate. Not yet, anyway. For the time being he'd enjoy the fact that he and his daughter shared something in common that could bring them closer together.

Mort did ask Rusty whether she'd heard about 92 burning down. She remarked that it was unfortunate for the owners, but she didn't harbour any personal feelings about the house one way or the other. "I left that part of my life behind a long time ago," she told her father.

Mort could have walked the two short blocks from his apartment on Peel Street to the El Morocco on Drummond, but making any extra effort to get to the restaurant seemed excessively conciliatory. Being in the car provided him excuses for temporarily staving off the inevitable. He circled the block, ostensibly looking for parking, but in reality enjoying listening to the Richard Harris cassette. He cruised along Sherbrooke Street, happily slowing to a stop at yellow lights about to turn red, and waiting for pedestrians to cross at their leisurely pace. He smiled at them as they strolled past his pouncing silver jaguar hood ornament. He contemplated saying to each pedestrian (for the first time in his fifty-odd years of driving) "take your time, no hurry at all." Turning the corner, he quickly located, to his dismay, a parking spot right in front of the restaurant. "Right when you *don't* want one," he muttered.

"Who puts a fancy restaurant on the ground floor of an apartment building, for crissakes?" Mort mumbled as he approached the entrance of the El Morocco. He remembered when *El Morocco* was the name of Montreal's hottest nightclub in the 1940s and '50s. It was managed by former NHLer Jimmy Orlando, and was where the biggest Hollywood stars of the day, Bing and Frank, cocktailed when they were in town. It was also the place at which the greatest burlesque star of the era, Lili St. Cyr, performed more than any other nightclub in town (they all wanted her) because she was Jimmy Orlando's girl.

Mort looked up at the *mezuzah* on the El Morocco's doorpost as he entered. The restaurant's decor looked kitschier than he had imagined it would: dimly lit, beige walls covered with mirrors in hammered brass frames and wall-hangings with arabesque designs surrounding ordinary-looking tables covered in white tablecloths and cheap wooden chairs. The ceiling drooped in swathes of drapery around light fixtures, and in the far corners of the room, Mort saw carpets on the floor and pillows scattered around midget tables. He imagined that he was about to enter a desert nomad's tent.

"How many?" said a smiling auburn-haired hostess dressed in a maroon satin caftan.

Five sheep and ten goats is my final offer, flashed through Mort's mind as an answer. "I'm meeting others," he said, squinting beyond the hostess to scan the restaurant's murky interior.

Most of the tables appeared to be occupied by families. There were few couples. The place was loud for an upscale establishment. It was not a Moishe's Steakhouse noise, or even a Schwartz's Hebrew Delicatessen racket, and certainly not the familiar, comforting din of Snowdon Deli. There were women and kid voices intermingled, bursts of laughter and exclamations, and all of it, in the breathy, slippery syllables of French. Mort was most definitely entering alien territory.

He didn't recognize any familiar hairdos or colouring. Mona's dyed-blond hair helmet could normally be seen in a crowd from a hundred feet away. And there was Gordon's dead giveaway head, his shiny bald pate wreathed in silver-hair with a white ponytail that hung down his back. Mort expected the ponytail to catch his eye like a swung lantern in the forest at dusk.

He'd always despised Gordon and not merely for his freeloading — he didn't have to see Mona's monthly bank statements to know that she (and, by alimony extension, he) was footing all their bills — but also for the snobbish way he dressed, the black turtlenecks and mohair, elbow-patched jackets. After all these years, Mort still could hardly believe that Mona had fallen for his befuddled academic schtick, the retired college English professor who might one day (because he still had it in him) write the great Canadian novel. Mort couldn't stand his nasal voice, either, and the way he spoke with a phony, slightly British accent. Everyone knew he was raised in working-class Verdun.

Gordon and Mona had met when he was the most popular book reviewer on the Hampstead circuit and Mona was the chairperson of her monthly book club. She was responsible for organizing the meetings and arranging guest speakers.

Mona had been divorced for a little over a year when word spread fast that she'd started dating Gordon. She was the envy of book-club ladies all over the city. As she tells it (Gordon never spoke publicly about such matters), he'd been smitten when Mona suggested that perhaps he'd been underselling himself all these years. Did he ever think, Mona asked, about starting a book review series? A hall could be rented and tickets sold. It would be a far more efficient and lucrative way of marketing and delivering his much sought-after services.

It didn't take much effort for Mona to persuade Gordon, who'd considered being outwardly entrepreneurial beneath him, to let Mona manage his career. She underwrote the venture, paying to rent a room with a podium and sound system in a hotel downtown while he prepared five book reviews. Advertisements were bought in *The Gazette* and press releases sent out to *The Suburban*, *The Monitor*, *The Canadian Jewish News*, and other community weeklies.

Word travelled quickly that Gordon Ash would no longer be visiting homes to deliver his book reviews. Before long, subscriptions to the first series were sold out. Another series of reviews had to be added and then a third to accommodate the demand. Soon there were two sets of three sold-out Gordon Ash Book Review Series, one in the fall and another in the spring. Shortly afterward, Toronto came calling, and Mona went about replicating her Montreal success with Gordon on the shores of Lake Ontario.

The Toronto move was crucial in ways that Mona could never have imagined. It brought Gordon to a whole new level of renown. He became the most famous book reviewer in the country, the main literary commentator on CBC radio, especially around literature awards season, which seemed increasingly to be all the time. A multiple book deal with the country's most prestigious publisher for hardcover compilations of Gordon's reviews followed. The Book Barn, the nation's largest chain of book discounters, featured a table of "Gordon Ash Recommendations" at the entrance of every store. Gordon was paid a monthly fee for the use of his name. And although several publishers had solicited his recommendation for a token "honourarium" — to be identified by a sticker in the upper right-hand corner on the cover of their new releases — Gordon had refused on the basis that his literary tastes were not for sale.

Whether their romance had blossomed from their business relationship or an instant attraction had sparked a desire to work together, one thing was sure, books had brought Mona and Gordon together, and for that alone, Mort loathed him.

Standing at the entrance of the El Morocco, looking for someone he might recognize, Mort suddenly felt overcome with exhaustion. He took a step backward, away from the hostess, and sat down in a seat by the door. He began to doubt whether he could go through with this.

Then, from within the restaurant's din Mort discerned the unmistakable baritone of Gordon's half-muted guffaw, like a splutter of water that suddenly bubbled up out of the fizzle of French chatter. The sound's origins were very close, seemingly right behind him. Mort turned his head and peered through a curtain of jangly beads next to his shoulder. He spied an alcove near the front door that he hadn't noticed earlier. It was a private space, slung with ceiling drapes, the floor covered in pillows in the traditional Moroccan style. For an instant it reminded Mort of a padded cell in an asylum.

And there was Gordon sitting cross-legged on a pillow and to his left, Mona. Jackie was next to Mona on her left. The boyfriend and his family sat across from Mona with their backs to Mort so he could not tell how they looked. Mort slunk down in his chair, careful not to be noticed by them through the curtain of beads.

He watched Jackie. His son hadn't changed much physically since the last time Mort had seen him. He looked healthy and tanned, though it may have been the darkness of the room. Jackie's hair was cut short and he was animated, smiling and gesturing extravagantly with his hands. He did indeed appear happy.

Gordon sat motionless, listening to the conversation swirling around him, looking authorial with his lips tightly locked, as if behind them a great utterance stirred and was dangerously on the verge of escaping lest he permit it.

But it was Mona that Mort was drawn to, sitting between the two men in her life. She wore a long African-patterned robe and her hair was covered by a multicoloured, silk kerchief. *She's dressed to fit in with the surroundings*, thought Mort. Mona's posture was square and her face more thickly jowled than he remembered. Her poise took Mort by surprise. She held herself with grace, a combination of serenity and nobility. And there was a certain strength too, a radiance that Mort could only describe as how a person looked when they had finally reached their destination. Mona was like a lioness surrounded by her pride. She made slight, self-contained gestures when she spoke. Her thin, manicured fingers rose to touch the underside of her chin below her ear, repeatedly stroking her neck. Mort couldn't take his eyes off his ex-wife. He let the seconds drain. The longer he stayed that way, immobilized and staring at her, the less he wanted to get up and join the party. It would be too much of an intrusion; upset the balance. Mona looked perfect the way she was. He didn't want to disrupt the tableau.

And then Mona seemed distracted, her eyes shifted as if she was looking for someone in the restaurant. An alarm had sounded in her mind. It was Mort she sought, wondering why he was so late. While the others talked, oblivious to Mort's absence, Mona grew more acutely aware of it and became increasingly distracted and less composed, stroking her neck nervously as if she was feeling for a gold necklace or an earring that was suddenly lost.

Mort could do one of two things, either enter the picture and screw things up even more, or just exit the restaurant quietly, unnoticed. If he left, there would be some discussion about why he hadn't shown up, and then after a few minutes they'd move on, enjoying themselves and their meal together. If he stayed and plopped himself down amongst them, there was no telling what he might say and who he might offend during dinner. He decided that it was probably a better idea to leave. He took one final look at Mona before slowly lifting his body and turning toward the exit. The glass door's hydraulic armature squeezed Mort out onto Drummond Street, but not before he glanced up at the *mezuzah* on the El Morocco's doorpost one last time.

six

Mort was feeling anxious when he entered his apartment and went straight for the living-room bar to pour himself the evening's first glass of Crown Royal. A shot or two of rye whisky would take the edge off. It always did. He'd left the restaurant to avoid screwing things up and turning the evening into a complete fiasco. Still, there were wounds that would have to be healed, hurt feelings and disappointments that would need consoling. Mort decided that he would call Mona later to explain and if required, apologize.

He poured himself the Crown Royal and walked over to the telephone answering machine, which was blinking red.

Beep. "Yes. Mr. Halbman. It's Officer Potente. Police arson investigations. We met briefly the other day at 92 Hampstead Road. Would you kindly call me back? I would very much appreciate a call. Thank you." A phone number was left at the end. Mort didn't write the number down on the pad sitting next to the answering machine. He remembered that he'd received Potente's business card and was pretty sure that it was still in the Jag. When the message ended a digital voice spoke up asking the listener if he wanted to erase the recording. Mort pressed Save just in case.

He walked over to his La-Z-Boy recliner, lowered himself slowly into it, and kicked up his legs carefully so as to avoid spilling the freshly poured whisky. He reached over and gently landed the glass on a booze stand, which was actually a carved wooden statuette of a slender, ample-breasted African woman holding a water jug on top of her head. It was a piece Mort had bought at a garage sale and modified to be his drink holder for TV-watching. It was probably not a good idea to return Potente's call this minute, he thought to himself. Potente had left an office number on the machine and it was well past business hours, anyway. Mort would call tomorrow.

He sipped his whisky. His final decisions for the day would entail whether to refill his glass once or twice after he drained the first, and how much TV he'd watch before heading off to bed. He picked up the remote and aimed it at the giant black rectangular screen that hung in the centre of his living-room wall and pressed two buttons. The screen lit up. He took double sips of whisky as pixilated images flicked across his field of vision. The last thing Mort remembered hearing before dozing off was the distant reverberation of laughter as if travelling into his mind from another dimension, and the sound of his involuntary chuckles and a disembodied voice, his own, responding "Stupid, stupid."

Beep. "Mort, you ol' stiff. Don't tell me you're out. Listen. I want to talk to you about Sandy. She's been asking about you again. I didn't want to say anything with the boys around the table at the del', but I need to talk to you. Call me."

Mort groggily opened his eyes and was momentarily blinded by a flood of light from the big-screen TV. He blinked and rubbed his eyes into focus, simultaneously smacking his tongue against the top of his mouth and swallowing repeatedly to kick-start his salivary glands into moistening his parched mouth.

It had sounded like Gerstein's nicotine-varnished pipes on the answering machine, but he couldn't be absolutely sure. He might have dreamed it. Mort heaved and groaned himself off the chair. The digital display flashed 9:43 p.m.. He pressed Play. It was Gerstein. He wanted to talk about Sandy. Mort hit Erase. He found the remote tucked into the corner of the La-Z-Boy and, in a sweeping motion of his arm, silenced the TV for the night with the pressure of his thumb.

Mort sat on his bed. He hadn't thought about Gerstein's sister for a while. He'd figured his friend had finally given up. Going all the way back to their Fairmount High days together and for as long as Mort had known him, the *yutz* had never been a quitter.

Sandy was still an attractive woman. She had kept herself in shape. The yoga clothes worn by Hampstead exercise-walkers her age made most of them look like pale, bulging knackwurst sausages wrapped in elastic bands. The tight, stretchy fabrics had inexplicably become popular, especially among women whose vintage flabbiness could ill afford such unforgiving fashion. On Sandy's lean physique, though, Lycra looked suitably sporty. Mort frequently saw Sandy and her cohorts pumping arms and legs and squaring their shoulders as they soldiered up the mountain like they were on patrol. Gerstein had mentioned to Mort that Sandy walked five miles every day. As if that weren't enough exertion, she followed it up by "climbing" for thirty minutes daily on an elliptical trainer in her den.

Sandy was among the new breed of Jewish women who were perpetually in training. They were like boxers preparing for a bout, getting in tip-top shape for going the inevitable twelve rounds toe-to-toe with the Big C, the undisputed, undefeated illness heavyweight champion of the world. Every August, Sandy and her speed-walking buddies raised the required two thousand dollars each for the privilege of marching sixty kilometres across the island of Montreal and back in the Jewish General Hospital's Weekend to End Breast Cancer. Each of them either knew someone who'd battled the disease, or felt that they were marked and had to do something "proactive" rather than sit around and wait to be struck down.

Sandy's conditioning, her regimen, advanced lung capacity, and increased stamina were hardly recommendations as far as Mort was concerned no matter how often Gerstein talked about it. They were part of the reason Mort could never imagine himself taking her out for dinner. Mort wondered if Sandy even ate dinner. Did she ever permit herself the indulgence of restaurant dining once in a while or was she always in training? Probably she fed herself like a rodent; handfuls of nuts and grains several times a day.

What interest, Mort asked himself, could a woman like Sandy possibly have in him? According to Gerstein she had been *interested* all these years and it had something to do with the kind of guy she thought Mort to be. Sandy had called Mort "good-hearted" and "true blue." *True blue*? Well, Mort decided, if she was misguided it was understandable given everything she'd been through.

Everyone in Côte Saint-Luc and Hampstead knew Sandy's story, Mort didn't have to hear it incessantly from Gerstein. At seventeen, Sandy (birth name: Shayndl) married twenty-two-year-old Chicky (birth name: Charles) Greenbaum of Greenbaum Pharmacies. It was a shotgun marriage, the result of Sandy's unwanted pregnancy, though the couple had successfully kept that fact secret from their respective families. Lucky for Chicky he was already working in the family business when Sandy got knocked up. He managed to get all the pregnancy tests done quietly so no one, not the parents, their closest friends, not even Rabbi Zelman, had the slightest inkling that Sandy was with child as they stood together under the *chuppah* at the Beth Zion Synagogue. Sandy didn't start showing until her sixth month.

The couple had three boys in four years and bought a semi-detached bungalow on Westluke Avenue. Fortunately, the Greenbaum Pharmacy chain expanded as fast as their family did. One modest outlet on Queen Mary Road soon became five spread out across the island. In a few years there were fifteen Greenbaum Pharmacies with stores as far away as Chicoutimi and Gaspésie. Chicky went from being in charge of shipping and receiving of their Montreal stores to director of purchasing and merchandizing for the whole chain. Buying trips followed with Chicky spending weeks at a time on the road checking up on stores.

The boys were six, seven, and eight when Chicky left on one of his regular business trips up north and didn't come back. He called Sandy from Lac Saint-Jean.

"There's someone else," he said.

Not suspecting a thing, she was stunned speechless.

"Pack me a valise. I'll be sending a guy from the office to pick it up."

"Who is it?"

"Someone here."

"What d'you mean *here?*"

"In Lac Saint-Jean. Manager of a Greenbaum's up here."

"*Putz.* How long has it been going on?"

"About three or four years. I've decided to stay."

"Prick."

"One more thing. You should know. We have a baby together."

The legal team of Greenbaum's Pharmacies had received more advanced notice of the news than Sandy. They managed to make it look like Chicky had been working as a clerk all these years and the judge bought it. Sandy didn't get a penny of alimony and only the bare minimum in child support payments.

Sandy was devastated and didn't date for years. Her exile was largely self-imposed. She knew that her story was making the rounds in the community and didn't want anybody's pity. It was doubtful whether many eligible men would want to date her, anyway. Instead, she concentrated her time and energy on rebuilding her life, setting it back on track, and devoting herself to the kids. She got a job working in real estate and went from a secretarial position to managing ten apartment buildings in less than two years. Gerstein helped his sister out, taking the boys out on weekends to Belmont Park, the Dow Planetarium, the Granby Zoo, and skiing in the winter. His devotion to his nephews was his way of positively channelling the murderous antipathy he felt toward his two-timing ex-brother-in-law. He was also hell-bent on eventually hooking Sandy up with one of his friends.

Gerstein claimed that he'd always known that Mort was perfect for his sister. After he split from Mona, and Sandy had mentioned Mort a few times, Gerstein decided he'd match them up if it was the last thing he did on earth. "I'm going to make the most perfect fucking *shidduch* between the two people I love the most in the whole goddamned world," is what Gerstein told Mort. And now that Gerstein was wearing a yarmulke under his Stetson and had become involved with a rabbi, Mort knew he would likely bring increased zeal to his campaign to bring him and Sandy together. Matchmaking had cosmic significance to the religious. Successful matches brought the matchmaker instant heavenly redemption. If Gerstein was serious about his turn to religion, Mort knew he was in deep trouble. Gerstein would be relentless, and he knew a thing or two about Gerstein's relentlessness. Sandy would not be the first time Gerstein had tried to fix Mort up with a girl.

It was Gerstein's idea to place the ad in the *Montreal Star*. He and Mort had already made a pact agreeing that they were both done with high school. They were fed up with meeting in the school library for detentions and decided that it was better to be out on the street, taking in some *real* action, making some dough. And anyway what further education did a kid need than ninth grade?

Gerstein had taken Mort aside and confided his secret plan, 'We'll get some fresh duds and hit the road like a coupla big shots."

Gerstein had always backed Mort into uncomfortable situations. At Fairmount High he'd been the kid who got his kicks publicly humiliating his closest friends. Mort was his favourite target. He'd be talking to a girl in the cafeteria or hallway and Gerstein would sneak up from behind, stick his face between them, and blurt out, "Morty was just telling me that he thought you had lovely buzoomers!"

In spite of his antics, Mort couldn't help liking Gerstein. He put up with the surprise attacks, got hot under the collar and red-faced, and then afterward they'd have a good laugh about it together. Mort never felt that Gerstein meant any harm by it. On some level he admired Gerstein for blurting out things he thought but would never dream of actually saying in public.

They were detention buddies. Mort would be kicked out of math class for doodling and Gerstein from English for talking out of turn. They'd meet in the library, Mort sitting quietly at a table drawing pictures on scrap paper and Gerstein blabbering on, ignoring the librarian's frequent shushing. Gerstein loved watching Mort draw. It was a consensus that Mort was the best artist in school. He could draw anything, real or imagined, from memory. In detention they played a game. Gerstein would challenge Mort to draw something outlandish, a penguin playing tennis, or an alligator playing ice hockey, and Mort would do it.

"Amazing!" Gerstein would declare.

"Now draw a picture of Mr. Grynzspan (Mort's despised math teacher) slapping Mrs. Findley (Gerstein's loathed English teacher) on the ass with a canoe paddle. And make her face look like she's *really* enjoying it."

Mort happily obliged.

"You know Halbman, you're a friggin Picasso," Gerstein would say, and Mort would quietly gloat.

Sitting in the library, there were times when Mort thought about being able to sketch anything he wanted from memory — any animal, face, activity, or setting — but being completely unable to remember math formulas, or memorize the multiplication tables. He came to the conclusion that it was because there were some things you remembered with your head, like numbers, and other things that you remembered with your heart, like shapes, colours, and shadows. He was a heart-memory type.

It was during their hours of detention in the library that the boys hatched an escape plan, and not just from detention, but from the whole scene that locked them in like a cage; from Fairmount High, from Montreal, from Canada. Within a week, they'd placed the advertisement in the *Star*:

Seeking ride to California, USA, or as close as possible. Willing to share the driving and expenses.

It didn't matter that neither Mort nor Gerstein had a driver's licence. At least Gerstein knew how. He'd been driving a car since he was eleven. His peddler father had taught him so that the boy could get behind the wheel of the Plymouth Deluxe on weekends when he went collecting from his accounts. With the seat cranked all the way forward, one foot barely touching the brake and his hands firmly on the Deluxe's large steering wheel, pre-pubescent Gerstein would ease the car forward along Saint-Dominique Street while his father climbed up and down stairs and knocked on doors. As Gerstein grew and his feet reached the pedals more easily, he was soon helping with his father's deliveries, too. By the time of his bar mitzvah he knew his father's entire route by heart and could run the business on his own if he had to.

To Mort, placing a classified ad was a lark. The phone number they'd put in the *Star* was Gerstein's and Mort didn't think much about it for the first few days. He nearly *plotzed* when, between classes, Gerstein grabbed him by the collar and dragged him into the boy's bathroom.

"What's the idea —"

"Cool down, brother." Gerstein smiled devilishly.

"No way." Mort's eyes swelled. He instantly knew what was coming.

"Uh-huh."

"You're kidding, right?"

"It's even better than we could've hoped for. A guy in a hurry. Taking his DeSoto into the States next week and looking for some company. Doesn't even want gas money."

"No!"

"Yep! Can you beat that?"

"Unbelievable."

Gerstein was elated and gung-ho. Mort was panicked. Escaping from Montreal was not an idea he'd ever really taken seriously. They were the wild machinations of two boys killing time in detention. Now that their fantasy was turning into reality, Mort didn't know what to do. He didn't want to leave his family, yet how could he back out on his best friend at this point? It was all happening too fast. Pondering his dilemma, Mort saw his high-school days slowly begin to recede. He realized that a die had already been cast — without his full consent. He wondered if this was the way it felt to grow up.

"Remember, we've got to look serious when the guy comes to pick us up. He asked me on the phone why we were going stateside. I told him that it was to pursue business opportunities. He wants to hit the road next Thursday. I told him that it was okay by us, the earlier the better. Of course, I was thinking that we'd have to sneak out. So I suggested that we leave at 4:00 a.m. when there's very little traffic across the bridge. He agreed. Seems like an okay fellow. Says he's going to visit family and is happy to have the company along for the ride. Mort, buddy, it looks like we're on our way!"

Mort wasn't listening to Gerstein. He was thinking about how he was going to break the news to his parents.

It didn't take long for him to decide that he couldn't say anything to them, at least not face to face. He'd leave a note. Something short and sweet. *Gone to California. Will call when we arrive ("we" because I'm going with Gerstein). I love you. Ma, please don't worry. We'll be fine. I swear it.*

Wheeling, West Virginia.

Three hours into their trip, immediately after the DeSoto crossed the United States border at Thousand Islands, the driver who called himself Rudy Snepps — a sharp-eyed, severe-looking, fedora-wearing fellow who'd made Mort jittery when he got into the car in the pitch black of early morning — revealed that he'd be dropping the boys off at Wheeling, West Virginia, and then continuing on alone southward toward Atlanta.

Hearing the news, Mort and Gerstein silently stared at each other, their heads spinning with exactly the same question: how close was Wheeling, West Virginia, to California? Very close, they hoped. Neither had the foggiest notion where on the map they were being deposited. California was itself not much more than an abstraction in their impressionable minds. It was a place on the other side of the North American continent with beaches, beautiful women, and Hollywood stars, where fortunes were made and dreams became reality. Staring at each other, in the front seat of Rudy Snepps's DeSoto, the boys wordlessly deliberated. Which one was going to speak up and ask the question? Fear won out over bravado.

"You mean you aren't driving to California?" Mort queried as politely as he could.

"Well, you did write in your *Star* advertisement that you wanted to go 'as close as possible,'" Snepps answered. "Wheeling is as close as my journey will take you. I'm sure you'll have no trouble finding other means to get you closer."

Gerstein interjected, "What's in Wheeling, West Virginia?"

"Not much. It's a small town. But I'll tell you what. You boys seem like mature, stand-up types. I have a dear old friend who lives in Wheeling. We'll head on over to his place to ask if he wouldn't mind putting you up for a couple of days while you find a ride west."

To say that Rudy Snepps made good on his word would be an understatement. The DeSoto pulled in through the gates of a castle on the outskirts of Wheeling. *Castle* was the word that came to Mort as he looked up through the car window at a series of nineteenth-century stone turrets.

"My friend likes his privacy. I'll go in and vouch for you. Wait here in the car until I get back."

Twenty minutes later, Mort could smell the odour of fine liquor and cigar smoke on Snepps's breath as he said, "You're all set, boys. You'll be staying in the guest house. Over there. And if I know my friend, you won't have to lift a finger."

A manservant approached the DeSoto to fetch the boys' valises from the trunk and carry them to a charming pitch-roofed dwelling to the right of the main house.

Mort watched the DeSoto kick gravel backward through the gate as it turned onto the main road. Silence settled around him and Gerstein as the car's dust trail cleared from the air.

Gerstein turned to Mort with the dumbest-looking clownish grin Mort had ever seen plastered across his friend's face. "Can you believe our luck?" Gerstein whooped, slapping Mort on the shoulder and dancing round him in a circle. "Will you look at this place?" He sang. "Just look at it," arms raised to the sky, hands spread wide like a hunter ritualistically thanking the gods for a successful kill. "Do we have it made or what?"

"What are you talking about? We're nowhere near California!"

They say that some people look at a glass and see it as half empty while others will regard the very same glass as half full. The glass Mort was looking at was neither half empty nor half full, it was just half way, and half way, he knew, was not close to how far Wheeling, West Virginia, was between Montreal and California. Another thing Mort could say with some certainty was that if his feelings about Gerstein were like a glass, it was rapidly filling up with doubt.

Gerstein twirled like a dervish. Mort watched him in silence, feeling numb. He knew that Gerstein's display was a pre-emptive strike of positive energy meant to counteract any possibility of hostility or despair that might be welling up inside Mort. But Gerstein needn't have worried. Mort was in the midst of an out-of-body experience, emotionally hovering somewhere between self-pity and bewilderment. After a few minutes, he gradually started returning to earth, his feet touching solid ground as his numbness dissipated into feelings of envy for the half-full glass from which Gerstein joyfully drank in the moment.

Mort and Gerstein never met the owner of the house, and never learned how the stranger had amassed his obvious fortune. Snepps hadn't been kidding when he said that the man liked his privacy. He'd not been seen around the grounds of the mansion during the entire time the boys were there. Nonetheless, the man, whoever he was, made sure that his guests were comfortable. His staff catered to their every need. Over the course of a week Mort and Gerstein were waited on, cooked breakfast, and served dinner. Their dwelling was cleaned by the housekeeping staff and their bedsheets and towels were changed daily. They even had a chauffeur driving them around. In hindsight, had Mort known the day they arrived about the boffo treatment they were in for, he wouldn't have let Gerstein dance alone. They would have danced the *hora* together, arm in arm.

Still, while Gerstein drank in the experience of being pampered with gusto, enjoying every minute of it, Mort remained wary. He wondered about what Snepps had told the owner about them. Had he lied and said they were big shots from Montreal, politicians, businessmen, or sons of British royalty? He couldn't imagine what he might have said that would have merited the VIP treatment they were receiving, and couldn't help wondering when and in what form repayment would be demanded. The answer came shortly.

Each night Mort and Gerstein went to a bar in town recommended by the manservant who'd been assigned to look after them. They spent liberally on drinks and cigars, feeling that they had to keep up the older, more mature and sophisticated image they were trying to cultivate. With the money they were saving money on room and board, they decided they could afford the indulgence. Going to the bar, Mort figured, was a good way of meeting folks and passing the word around that they were looking for a ride out west.

One evening, a startling woman dressed to the nines, with flowing black hair and fire-engine-red lipstick, was sitting at the bar. Watching her out of the corner of his eye, Gerstein noticed that the woman periodically lifted her head up from the bar to stare over at Mort. Mort, of course, denied noticing anything, until Gerstein, who relished such situations and was more than slightly inebriated, said, "Well, if you won't do anything about it then I certainly will."

Here it comes, thought Mort.

Gerstein marched over to the woman and invited her to join them at their table. Mort watched, expecting her to hesitate at the request. She did nothing of the sort. She rose effortlessly from her barstool and, with Gerstein gleefully trailing behind, cruised in high heels and stockings toward Mort. Without a word, she lowered herself into the seat beside him and simultaneously slid her almost empty glass along the table, clinking it against Mort's half-filled whisky.

"Barkeep, bring the lady another drink," Gerstein shouted toward the bar as if he expected to be heard.

"Where're you gentlemen from?" The woman asked, looking at Mort.

"Back east," Gerstein piped in before Mort could speak.

"So you're here for the races?"

"That's right," Gerstein said, looking straight at Mort, signalling with his eyes to follow his lead.

"Well you're lucky. The weather's been perfect."

"Nothing like the races when the weather's perfect," Gerstein said, nodding his head.

Mort nervously sipped the last of his whisky.

"Here are the passes," the woman said opening her purse and extracting two playing-card-size tickets. She handed them to Mort. "Tomorrow at noontime present yourselves at Gate 34 behind the stables. I'll meet you to take you up to our private box in the clubhouse."

The woman stood up. "I look forward to seeing you."

Gerstein could barely contain his excitement for the balance of the evening. "It's been arranged by our host," he reassured Mort, who looked at the passes suspiciously. "Who else would have a private box in the clubhouse? You heard what she said: '*our* private box.' This is just one more way of showing their hospitality. Man, do I ever love it here in Wheeling, West Virginia. Wonderful Wheeling, West Virginia! And to think we'd never even heard of this place!"

What Mort heard that gave him pause was the word 'the' when she handed them the passes. She hadn't said *some* passes, but *the* passes as if she thought the boys expected them. Mort mentioned his thought to Gerstein, but the only thing that mattered to him at the moment was that they were going to see thoroughbred horses race the next day. Neither had ever been to the racetrack before, though Montreal did have the Hippodrome up on Decarie Boulevard. It only took a couple more whiskies for Mort's hesitation to wear off. Mort would trace his lifelong taste for whisky to that week in the Wheeling bar.

The next day the boys were chauffeured to the Wheeling Racetrack at the appointed hour, as instructed. The woman from the bar was there to meet them. She led them through Gate 34 behind the stables and into the clubhouse. From there they climbed stairs to a private box in the viewing stand that overlooked the racetrack.

It was a bright day and Mort was instantly awed by the breathtaking sight that greeted him: a hoof-pocked soil track ringing a white, fenced-in oval of grass. He knew that momentarily, the stuttered call of trumpets would summon a procession out onto the track, magnificently muscled, statuesque beasts, their faces masked, tails flicking to and fro behind them, with helmeted midgets garbed in multicoloured silks astride them, reins in hand, but looking as comical as circus monkeys. At that moment, the horse race seemed less like a sporting event than the staging of some extravagant pagan ritual.

It was the grounds themselves that drew and kept Mort's attention. The inherent serenity of the architecture, the combination of earthy browns and grassy greens, instantly reminded him of Delormier Downs where the Montreal Royals played baseball: a sun-dappled field touched by a palette of yellows and oranges and blues, and the infield diamond shaping exquisite geometry into inner and outer forms, imagined sanctums.

Mort saw that three other men were already seated at tables in the private box. Drinks were being served to them by a waiter. Mort relished having a couple of whiskies to enhance the already intoxicating view he was enjoying from his clubhouse perch.

As soon as they were seated, the beautiful black-haired woman approached.

"You better hurry," she said, dropping another card, this one business-card size, on the table in front of Gerstein.

In hushed tones, as if he was sharing a secret, Gerstein read to Mort a series of numbers. They were betting numbers. And since neither of them had ever bet on horses before, they followed the lead they were handed by walking over to a man in a glass booth they'd seen outside the private box, and uttered the numbers off the palmed card.

"How much?" The man wanted to know.

"What?"

"How much do you want to bet?"

"Oh. Yeah." Gerstein turned to Mort to deliberate.

"Two bucks," Gerstein announced.

"Two bucks?"

"Yeah, two. Here's two smackeroos," Gerstein said importantly, slapping the bills down.

The numbers they bet in the first race came in. The payoff was eight dollars. "Beginner's luck," Gerstein said to Mort.

When they got back to their table they had drinks waiting for them. Moments later, the beautiful black-haired woman was back with another business card. The boys returned to the betting window.

"How much this time?" Gerstein giddily whispered to Mort like he'd discovered the secret to eternal life.

"Let's do five?" Gerstein suggested. "I'm still feeling lucky."

Mort nodded his agreement.

"Five bucks," Gerstein shouted into the window, followed by the numbers he'd memorized off the card.

Back at their table, another card was waiting for them. Only this time it had numbers for the next five races.

Their numbers came in again for the second, third, fourth, and every subsequent race. Each time Mort and Gerstein bet the winnings from the previous race. According to Mort it made sense to use that betting system. This way they would always be ahead of the game even if they lost. With every victory Gerstein whooped it up louder and louder, hollering "Wonderful Wheeling,

West Virginia! Wonderful Wheeling, West Virginia!" The men they were sharing the private box with seemed to be enjoying a miraculous spate of good luck, too, but were less demonstrative in their cheer. Mort watched them count fat wads of bills each time they returned from visiting the betting wicket between races. By the fourth race the men weren't watching the horses at all, let alone cheering on their picks, just counting their cash.

The boys' winnings totalled five hundred dollars when the day was done. "Hey, if we see the woman who fed us the numbers, why don't we give her a nice tip," Mort suggested to Gerstein.

"What do you mean, like fifty bucks?"

"No, you *schnorrer*, like a hundred," Mort said. "We're taking home five hundred. It's the least we can do. The balance will help us get to California."

The boys didn't have to look far for the beautiful black-haired woman. She met them after the races outside the gate. Pulling up in a Packard Clipper she rolled down her window and invited them in for a ride home.

"Have a good time boys?"

"Sure did!" said Gerstein confidently.

"Glad to hear it."

"Thanks for the tips!"

"Pleasure."

Mort said, "My friend and I were thinking that you'd appreciate a small token of our gratitude."

"Gladly," the woman said as she casually pulled the Packard over to the side of the road.

Gerstein counted out ten ten-dollar bills and handed them to the woman.

"What the hell is this?" she asked, looking at her hand.

"Just to show our appreciation," Gerstein smiled.

"Are you nuts? Who the hell do you think you are? They told me that you were players from back east. What kind of game is this? Didn't you bet?"

"Surely, we bet," said Mort. "We're offering you a good portion of our winnings."

"You gotta be kidding," the woman said. "Just get the hell out of my car! Right now! And if you know what's good for you you'd better pack your things and get out of town before nightfall!"

"What's the big idea?" Gerstein exclaimed, wiping his brow with his jacket sleeve and staring at the Packard's parking lights as they sped off down the road. "What did she mean by 'you better get out of town if you know what's good for you'? Who does she think *she* is?"

"Don't you get it?" Mort said later, as they dragged themselves miserably along the road toward the centre of town, the late afternoon sun wetting the backs of their necks.

"Get what?"

"The fix was in. Don't tell me you couldn't figure that out?"

"Yeah. Of course, I figured as much," Gerstein said. "But you have to admit, we sure got it good. Who'd that broad think she was, anyway?"

"We were stooges," Mort said. "They expected us to bet like big shots and give her the lion's share of the winnings, thousands, even tens of thousands, not a hundred bucks. Man, are we ever big *schmucks* not big *shots*. We were ripe. That's what Snepps must have told his friend. Putting us up at the mansion, the chauffeur, the butler, it was all part of the scheme. Real high-class *schmucks*, that's what we are."

"Well, look at this way, Morty. We're four hundred bucks richer. Nothing to sneeze at. Now we have enough to get us to California by bus."

"Yeah, the faster we get out of here the better. Three cheers for 'Wonderful Wheeling, West Virginia,'" Mort said sarcastically.

"Wonderful Wheeling, West Virginia."

The phrase repeated itself in Mort's whisky-addled brain as he sat on the edge of his bed and thought about all the crazy situations he'd allowed Gerstein to corner him into since they were fifteen years old. "Wonderful Wheeling, West Virginia" became their private code for good luck that suddenly turned sour, or sure bets that ended up biting them in the ass. Whenever Gerstein came up with a cockamamie idea he would say to Mort, "Don't chicken out on me now, Halbman. Remember Wonderful Wheeling, West Virginia." And it didn't take long for Mort's doubtful scowl to turn into a smile and he was playing a role in Gerstein's plan no matter how far-fetched. Mort wondered if hooking him up with Sandy was another one of Gerstein's crazy schemes.

seven

Intense strategizing preceded the return call. Should he phone at
the end of the day when the recipient would be fatigued from long
hours of activity and perhaps slightly unguarded? Or might he
receive a fresher, more upbeat reception in the morning, the first
coffee's bitterness still on the answering voice's lips, a jolt of sugar
juicing the bloodstream, and the onslaught of the day's inevitable
mayhem not yet underway? Which would give him a better chance
of easing the discussion in a favourable direction? He would be
congenial throughout no matter which way the conversation was
headed, that much he had already decided. His tone would remain
steady and affable to the point of cheery. Given the opportunity,
what angle should he take? He could plead ignorance. It had
worked before. Or would it be better to accept some responsibility
for his behaviour? To show that he was a reasonably aware
individual who took consequences seriously. And there was the
crucial matter of where he would place the call from. The location
seemed to him now to be mortally important. Wherever it was it
had to be from somewhere he felt completely comfortable.

Mort owed a call to Mona, apologizing for not showing up at the restaurant, and one to Gerstein to explain why he couldn't have dinner with Sandy. It was the call to Officer Massimo Potente that prompted the self-interrogation. Each phone call required its own strategy and manoeuvering. Mort felt apprehensive. When had every phone call become equally fraught with hazard? Old buddies, ex-wives, and police arson investigators had suddenly become undifferentiated, each an ingredient in the stew of anxiety that was his life.

Okay. Enough fretting. Decisions had to be reached. First, about the location where he would place the call to Officer Potente. It didn't take Mort very long to decide on the Jag, the comfort of his luxury vehicle. He'd spoken with Potente before from the Jag outside 92 Hampstead Road. That time he'd held his conversational ground. The Jag was also where he'd find the officer's business card with his phone number on it.

The omens, however, did not appear to be in Mort's favour. Initially, it came as a feeling of general unease that grew inside him as he made his way down to his parking spot on the second level of his building's four-tiered garage. Something was amiss. He could sense it in his bones, the clamminess of his hands. To reassure himself, he felt for the cellphone and car keys in his jacket pocket. They were there.

Mort approached the Jag, its molded rear bumpers and rounded wheel wells looking from behind like a jungle cat's muscular haunches in the resting position, a double-barreled exhaust-pipe like a thick, feline tail peeking out underneath. Mort jiggled the keychain in his hand as he removed it from his pocket. Pointing the device in the general direction of the vehicle, he pressed a button to emit an inaudible command. The Jag winked its headlights as if blinking eyes after a lazy afternoon nap and then made a soft squeak like the end of a waking yawn. Door locks clicked open automatically in unison.

Mort opened the driver's side door as much as his narrow

parking space would allow. The edge scraped the concrete pillar for the hundredth time, chipping the metallic paint. For over a decade Mort had lobbied, first the management, and then the tenant's association board of directors, to have his parking spot moved to somewhere more accessible on the first level. He appealed to their sense of compassion, claiming that persistent health problems (rheumatism in the ankles and occasional bouts of gout) required that he have a parking spot closer to the elevators. He even tried to bribe the association president to no avail; a cash gift in an envelope at holiday time with a card inscribed, "a token of appreciation for all the good work you have been doing on behalf of tenants such as myself." Unlike jumping the queue in the hospital for quicker service, a better parking spot in his apartment building could not be bought.

Mort had been refused a dozen times in total. The official reason was that the closer spots were reserved for handicapped parking and residents who had seniority. He'd have to be patient like everyone else for a spot to become available. But one never did. The real reason, he knew, was prestige and status. The cars populating the garage's first level belonged to legislators, diplomats, judges, and CEOs. His Jag would not have been out of place amid their BMW, Mercedes-Benz, and Lexus vehicles, but *he* would have. Mort had come to the conclusion that he would have to be satisfied with making it up to the second level from the fourth where he'd started when he first moved in to the building after divorcing Mona. Sliding his girth sideways and dropping into the Jag's leather seat Mort simultaneously cursed, sighed, and groaned.

The Jag purred alive. Mort backed the car slowly out of its narrow spot and piloted it through the zig-zag of ramps up through the building's cavernous substructure and into daylight. He turned south on Peel. The fireball sun rose above the horizon at the bottom of the street. Mort faced directly into it. Shards of sunlight ricocheted off the tinted glass of the bordering office towers, forcing Mort to shield his eyes with his left hand while maintaining the right on the steering wheel. At the stoplight on René Lévesque Boulevard, Mort realized he was heading in the wrong direction. He didn't want to be going south toward Old Montreal and the Port. He needed to be driving north, up the mountain, to the lookout. There, above the hubbub of downtown morning rush-hour traffic, it would be quiet and he'd be able to talk with Officer Potente in peace. Even better, he'd have a view of the Olympic Stadium in the distance.

It didn't matter what had been said over the years about "The Big O." Mort didn't care that it had been maligned for being poorly constructed, awkwardly designed, and basically unsuitable for sporting events. Sure, he'd felt resentment and anger along with every other Montreal taxpayer over the multi-billion dollar debt that had been incurred to build the stadium. He too had felt contempt for the corruption and incompetence of the politicians, bureaucrats, and contractors. The Big O was unarguably a folly, a white elephant that had validly been the butt of a million jokes for decades. Mort had laughed and cried and been outraged along with all Montrealers.

But bygones were bygones. The building was finally paid off after more than a generation of shelling out. Mort was feeling a special connection to the stadium lately, a kind of affection mixed with nostalgia; in a word, kinship. Since the Expos had been shipped off to Washington, the stadium sat unwanted, unappreciated, and generally unused, except for the odd convention, trade show, or steroidal monster-truck extravaganza. To Mort, The Big O would forever remain the Expos' final home, the last place they played in Montreal, and therefore the team's final resting place: sacred ground. The history embodied by the place was irrevocable, both the good and bad, the glory and shame, though Mort would always focus on the moments of splendour. And there had been many. He could cite them from memory, chapter and verse. He'd been there in person to witness them all.

The early years at the Olympic Stadium were particularly auspicious. Mort could tell anyone that the first home run hit by the Expos at the Olympic Stadium was on April 15, 1977, in the second inning against the Philadelphia Phillies by outfielder Ellis Valentine. Mort had been at the Big O in 1978, their second season after moving from Jarry Park, when Ross Grimsley became the first and only Expos pitcher to win twenty games in a season. Mort saw shortstop Chris Speier become only the second Expos player ever to hit for the cycle (single, double, triple, home run) at the stadium on July 20, 1978. He was there the very next season when the team challenged for the divisional title, finishing only one game behind the eventual World Champion Pittsburgh Pirates. Mort was at the game on May 10, 1980, when Expos pitcher Charlie Lea no-hit the San Francisco Giants. Later that season, on September 10, he watched Bill Gullickson set a National League rookie record with eighteen strikeouts against the Chicago Cubs, a record that would stand for eighteen years. Mort was at the Olympic Stadium on July 13, 1982, for the first-ever Major League Baseball All-Star Game held outside the United States. Five Expos were on the National League squad that year, Andre Dawson, Gary Carter, Tim Raines, and Steve Rogers as starters, and slugger Al Oliver in reserve. That was the year Oliver became the first Expo to win a National League batting title with a .331 average, and Mort had witnessed so many of his at-bats. Mort was also there when Tim Raines became the second Expo to win a batting title in 1986 with a .334 average. He was at the game on April 13, 1984, when baseball's greatest hitter, Pete Rose, while playing for the Expos, became only the second slugger in history (with legendary Ty Cobb) to have four thousand hits. During the 1985 season, Mort had seen Expos reliever Jeff Reardon lead the league in saves. He'd stayed for every minute of the twenty-two-inning marathon that the Expos played against the Los Angeles Dodgers at the Big O on August 23, 1989, the longest game in club history. Mort remembered that game less for the final score (the Expos lost) than for their giant, lovable, furry mascot Youppi! getting ejected by the umpire, also a Major League first.

The most unforgettable and bittersweet memory of all was the 1994 season, the season of heartbreak. The playoff-bound Expos had a league-best record of seventy-four wins and forty losses in August and were on track to win over one hundred games for the first time in their history until the entire season was wiped out by a player's strike. That was the year *Nos Amours* would have made it to the World Series, and probably would have won it all. Mort had attended most of their home games, and, sensing history was in the making, had recorded every out, walk, and hit. When the players strike was announced on August 12, 1994, his heart dropped in his chest. He knew instinctively that it would be the Expos' last chance. The club would never fully recover. And he was right. There were other highlights in later seasons: Pedro Martinez's Cy Young Award as the National League's best pitcher in '97 and Vlad Guerrero's 42 homers in '99, to name only two. But the stolen World Championship, the championship that should have been, but never was, eclipsed them all.

The lookout at the top of Mount-Royal was empty, just as Mort had predicted. The last of the lovers who traditionally came to watch the sunrise over the city were gone. A veil of dew hung in the air and the ambient hum of traffic gently rolled up the mountain's rocky eastern slope. Mort opened the compartment between the Jag's front seats. Officer Potente's business card was exactly where he'd left it. He picked it up and simultaneously extracted the cellphone from his jacket pocket.

When Mort looked out through the Jag's front windshield, the massive white lump of the Big O glowed eerily in the distance at the island's east end. It looked like an enormous mound of sun-bleached elephant bones. The monumental inclined tower that loomed above the stadium's roof was a colourless oblong slab. Mort imagined it as an uprooted, leaning headstone on which the Expos logo was engraved in grey concrete with the years *1969–2004*.

Whatever anyone might say about the stadium, there it was. An undeniable fact. An indelible part of the city and its story. To hold the incompetence and foolishness of its creators against it would be like blaming an orphaned child for its birth. The Olympic Stadium was a part of Mort and all Montrealers, and, as such, forever their collective responsibility, like the gravesite of a deceased relative that needed care and regular tending in perpetuity. Demolishing the stadium to build condos or affordable housing as some had advocated was, as far as he was concerned, a desire to rid Montrealers of not just the stadium's physical presence, but also of what it represented, a chapter of the city's past. To Mort such an act would constitute a crime against history and memory.

Mort began dialling Officer Potente's number on his cellphone. He was halfway done when, looking out at the Olympic Stadium in the distance, his focus shifted inward the way a marksman's aiming vision might shift toward the crosshairs on his rifle.

Mort noticed the ornament on the Jag's hood. Or rather he noticed its absence. He cancelled his call and heaved himself out of the car, dragging his body along the Jag's hood toward the front. The lithe, sleek, pouncing, silver Jaguar was gone. Stolen. Literally ripped off. All that remained was a hole in the tiny, round podium where the Jaguar's paws had been affixed to the car's hood. Mort stared into the hole for a minute, feeling disappointed rather than enraged. He didn't have the energy for rage. "Punks and hoodlums," he muttered disgustedly under his breath. If the car had been parked on the first level of the garage near the elevators this would never have happened. At the next tenant's association meeting he'd insist on a better parking spot. Meanwhile he wondered what a new ornament might cost. A small fortune, no doubt. Maybe he could find a used one.

Back in the car, Mort stared out through the windshield and felt resigned. He thought about all the things he'd taken for granted, even something as stupid as the little Jaguar hood ornament, and now it was gone. He looked at Officer Massimo Potente's card and dialled the number on his cellphone, still feeling unprepared. It was a direct line. No answering machine asking you to press more buttons to get you to your eventual destination. Mort was slightly relieved not to have to deal with navigating through an automated phone system.

"I'm pleased to hear from you," Potente said. "Thank you for returning my call so quickly." Mort asked the officer if it was necessary to meet in person.

"No, it's okay. Not at this juncture."

What exactly did he mean by "this juncture"?

"I was calling for some follow-up to our meeting at 92 Hampstead Road. Some information that came to light that I wanted to ask you about, if you don't mind?"

No. Of course, not.

"I had the opportunity to speak with Mrs. Halbman."

Who? Mrs. Halbman?

"We spoke briefly about 92 Hampstead Road."

Mona.

"I noticed that she was the deed-holder who had sold the house to the Shines. We spoke about your time in the house. When you were married."

Mort interrupted. "Officer Potente, may I ask you a question?"

"Certainly."

"Why would you be interested in my marriage?"

"Well, it's not your marriage, exactly, that is germane to our investigation."

Mort momentarily felt relief.

"In my line of business, we like to get to know as much as possible about a house, and a lot can be learned from its history. I like to be as thorough as possible which means starting at the very beginning, going back to the building of the structure, how it was constructed, the blueprints if possible. You were, in fact, directly involved in the design and construction of the house, were you not?"

Feeling complimented, Mort was about to answer that indeed he'd had a direct hand in the design, insisting on various architectural elements, including a one-of-a-kind stone fireplace, but stopped himself. "Okay," was all he said.

"Well then, perhaps you would know more than anybody, with the exception of the architect himself — a Mr. Shritz, I believe — about the materials that went into the house, the type of wood and stone, the electrical wiring, the studding, the type of insulation, that sort of thing, and especially about the design. These all play significant roles in how a home burns."

I see.

"But I must say that Mrs. Halbman had other interesting things to share."

Oh, really.

"She mentioned an incident —"

An incident? Mort paused, thinking for a moment. *There were moments in a person's life ...* The phrase inexplicably popped into his head, blotting out Potente's next sentence the way a passing siren interrupts part of a song playing on the car radio. *There were moments in a person's life ...* he mentally repeated and listened for the phrase to finish; *that instantly made sense of everything.* No. *That brought everything full circle.* No. *That backed you into a corner and forced you to acknowledge that nothing was in your control and your life was a just a great big sham, a shambles.* None of these phrases adequately finished the mysterious sentence.

Mort had lived a fairly ordinary life. Not a particularly reflective or passionate one, except for his love of the Expos, and the other great passion of his life: the house he'd helped to design and build on Hampstead Road in 1969. Suddenly, he had a realization. It was as obvious as a blizzard in January and yet, somehow, he'd never seen it. 92 Hampstead Road was built the very same year the Expos had played their first home game at Jarry Park. He could not believe that this coincidence had never occurred to him before and wondered about its significance.

"I'm sorry, Officer Potente. You said something about an incident?"

"Nothing terribly important, really. Just something Mrs. Halbman mentioned. She humorously called it 'cooking the books.'"

Now Mort knew how the phrase that had popped inexplicably into his mind was supposed to end: *There were moments in a person's life when their single greatest accomplishment came round to bite them on the ass.*

Mort had wanted a fireplace. He'd insisted on one to Shritz, but not just any regular fireplace. Not a flimsy prefabricated one, or one made of brick with a wood mantel. Mort's fireplace had to be made of solid stone through and through, five feet thick. And not just a fireplace with one opening, but four, a single exposed structure with multiple openings that went from the basement all the way up to the chimney in one piece. It would be the centrepiece of the home, the structure around which the rest of the house would stand: the focal point, like the altar inside a religious temple. The location and orientation of the bedrooms, kitchen, living room, and dining room, would be determined by its proximity to the fireplace. Shritz had asked why. Why so much emphasis on the fireplace? And why four openings, two upstairs and two downstairs? This was not the olden times when you needed a fireplace to provide heat, or for cooking. A typical modern family dwelling needed only one fireplace, and even then, only for decorative or recreational purposes.

Mort insisted that his fireplace not be "decorative" or "recreational." It would be the very heart of his home. The fireplace would open to the living room on one side and through to the dining room on the other. A fire lit inside would burn vibrant and orange, visible from both sides at once. It was an idea that had possessed Mort with a fervour, fired his imagination, and drove him to find the discarded stone that he needed from the University of Montreal sports complex construction site up on Mount-Royal.

But, like many obsessions, the thrill was extinguished almost as soon as it became a reality. Mort blamed it on Mona. From the day they'd moved in she didn't care for the fireplace. It took up too much room, she complained. The exposed stone gathered dust. Grains of cement from the mortar holding the irregularly shaped rocks together peppered the floor and had to be swept up all the time. She hated the mess made by the cords of wood Mort bought from a Laurentian supplier and stacked along a wall in the garage. He'd schlep the chopped wood into the house and dump it in little piles next to the fireplace that annoyed Mona to no end. She said that no one, least of all her, was going to waste an afternoon sitting around a fire. She was wrong. Mort did. That first winter he made a fire most evenings after work, and every Sunday he'd spend several hours staring into the shifting flames. It brought him a sense of peace and tranquility. Mort even tried to keep the fireplace burning into the spring. But by May of that first year living at 92, the hearth was cold. It remained barren for the next sixteen years up until the day Mort left for good, almost without interruption.

The fireplace was called briefly back into service during the early years. It was not for lighting fires, though. Jackie was attending Notre-Dame de Sion pre-school on Queen Mary Road near Saint Joseph's Oratory. Run by nuns dressed in large, black, hooded habits, the pre-school had inexplicably become trendy among the *nouveau riche* Jewish families of Hampstead.

One day Jackie came home from school and asked Mona why they didn't hang stockings on their fireplace at Christmastime like the other families did. "Why else have a fireplace?" he questioned understandably since he had never seen a fire there. Priding herself on being open-minded, Mona considered her son's query carefully and decided that he had a point. There was, in fact, no good reason not to hang stockings from the fireplace. It would be a clean and enjoyable purpose for the otherwise useless household feature. On Christmas Eve, at Mona's insistence, Mort found himself rushing out to the neighbourhood pharmacy to buy mesh plastic stockings filled with candies and cheap Taiwan-made novelties for Jackie and his baby sister Rusty. This was the price he'd have to pay for keeping the peace at home, Mort told himself. His child would avoid disappointment and be able to tell his goyish school friends that he too had received gifts from Santa Claus.

Thankfully, Mona never insisted on a Christmas tree or Channukah bush for the kids. Mort had already decided that the stockings were where he would draw the line. He also decided that there was no way Jackie was staying at the nun-run school. His boy's future non-Jewish expectations would be curtailed by immediate removal and enrollment in the Jewish People's School on Van Horne. Jackie and Rusty would spend thirteen years of their adolescent lives learning Jewish traditions, Bible, and how to speak, read, and write in Hebrew and Yiddish. Mort convinced himself that learning Yiddish, especially, the medieval language of his Ashkenazi ancestry, a language which he himself was unable to speak, was sure to inoculate his kids against any further goyish influences and desires. Thinking about it now, he credited the decision to enroll his kids in a Jewish day school as the determining factor for their decisions to marry Jews; in Rusty's case a religious Jew, which was marginally preferable to marrying a secular non-Jew, and in Jackie's, a gay Jew, which was significantly preferable to a gay non-Jew.

When Mort thought about the fireplace now, his stomach cramped up in response to one more memory.

In the year or two following his divorce, he'd invited Jackie out to dinner at the Rib and Reef on Decarie Boulevard, a well-known Garmento hangout with excellent surf and turf. Mort was trying to keep the father-son channels open the only way he knew how, by inviting his indifferent son out to dinner and *schtupping* him with cash. This was before the mortgage business. Jackie was nineteen and living in a rented two-room apartment on Sherbrooke and Girouard. Mort had heard from Mona that he was hard up, having just lost his sales job at a clothing store downtown.

At the restaurant, father and son talked uncomfortably over drinks, live piano-bar music from the next room providing background. Each struggled to find something to say that might establish a connection. Staring into his glass of gin and tonic, Jackie finally smiled and said, "You know Dad, one of the fondest memories I have of being at home?" Mort grinned and eased back in his chair, feeling like a centrefielder waiting under a pop-fly, certain that he was perfectly set for the ball to drop right into the pocket of his mitt.

"What's that, son?" he said.

"The way we'd come downstairs on Christmas morning and find stockings filled with candy hung over the fireplace."

In the years Mort lived at home, his disappointments had accumulated inside and seeped out like visible wood rot. All of his repressed resentment and hostility eventually had to combust. In retrospect, it was the only explanation Mort could come up with for why, one day, he went downstairs to his workroom, and, like a child bent on knocking down a rival child's toy blocks, took apart Mona's collection of self-help books stack by stack.

Mort didn't stop there. He decided he had to be rid of the books once and for all. He carried armfuls, a dozen at a time, upstairs and placed them in neat piles next to his fireplace until the massive stone structure was framed in tall paperback columns. Then Mort stoically lit a match and held it to the thin, beige cover of the worn, dog-eared volume lifted from the top of the stack, a book entitled *Too Good For Your Own Good*. The book was set alight easily, as if it had waited anxiously for this day to come and wanted to burn.

Mort placed the flaming book in the fireplace and calmly took more books off the stack like they were blocks off a woodpile, laying them one at a time into the hearth in formation, careful to leave enough room for the flames to breathe. He soon learned that to grow the flames it helped to open the books like birds with spread wings, or tear pages out in fistfuls like tufts of plucked feathers to sprinkle on the devouring flame. The fire grew redder and hotter and was quickly able to consume books whole. Mort tossed them in one by one. The flames were ravenous for Mona's library, and with each additional volume the inferno became more intense, filling Mort's fireplace with a kaleidoscope of flickering oranges, yellows, whites, and blues. It was exactly the kind of fire he'd always wanted and dreamed of when he was building the house. He basked in the swelling heat. As the library turned to glowing embers and ashes, Mort felt somehow relieved, unburdened, cleansed. It did not occur to him until months later, when Mona had filed for divorce and he'd received the legal papers, that his act was worse than just an offense against his wife, the person to whom the books belonged and who'd cherished them. It was much worse. It was a sacrilege. He was a Jew who had burned books.

Mort hadn't given any thought to the possibility that his plan could backfire. Lighting up a fireplace for the first time after many years of disuse could present unforeseen complications. In this case, the flue was rusty and could only be opened partially. Mort had turned the handle as far as it would go. As books burned and the flames gained momentum, multiplied, and rose, smoke gradually began backing down the chimney into the living room. Only when Mona's library had been about 10 percent incinerated did Mort realize the air inside his home had thickened. He felt a tickle in the back of his throat and was soon buckled over in a fit of coughing.

Mort had always assumed that his neighbours were respectful of privacy and minded their own business. He'd considered it an entitlement of living in a better neighbourhood where the houses were large and spread out. It was doubly surprising then, that even before the first fire trucks arrived, a trio of neighbours gathered along the sidewalk outside his front door to gawk. Bernie Mandelbaum was implausibly already waiting on the sidewalk outside Mort's front door when he staggered out coughing and gagging. Bernie smiled at Mort reassuringly and told him not to worry because he'd already called the firemen. They were on their way and should appear any second. Harvey Hart said the same thing to Mort. Completing the sidewalk triumvirate was Murray Shostak.

A full scale tragedy was averted. Using a simple wrench — not even "the jaws of life" or some such specialized gadget — the firemen managed to twist the flue completely open and let the smoke escape. Mort was grateful that they weren't an axe- or hose-happy bunch. This crew was most probably specially trained to take extra care of property; another benefit of living in ritzy Hampstead.

Notwithstanding the embarrassment he'd endured in front of his neighbours that day, Mort's only lasting regret was not getting the chance to finish the job. He thought about it for months afterward, especially during the divorce proceedings. There were so many of Mona's books he hadn't had the time to pile into his prized fireplace before being overcome by smoke.

"There's a record of the call at Hampstead Fire Department. Trucks from stations in Côte Sainte-Luc and Notre-Dame-de-Grâce were also involved, I believe."

"Surely, Officer Potente, you don't think that because my ex-wife and I had a little domestic scrap many years ago, I'm linked to the recent fire on Hampstead Road?"

"No, of course not. But there's a history of fire in the house, which is always intriguing."

Mona could never forgive me.

"The way Mrs. Halbman called it 'cooking the books' really made me laugh — made it stick in my mind."

And now she's seized on an opportunity for revenge.

"It's a euphemism for setting a fire I'd never heard before. Where I grew up in Saint Leonard, do you know what we used to call arson for the purposes of collecting on an insurance policy? And please don't take this personally, Mr. Halbman."

Mort knew.

"Jewish lightning."

Fucking wop.

eight

Mirtcha had a candy store
Business it was bad.
He asked a friend what to do
And this is what he said.

Take a can of gasoline
Shmear it on the floor.
Take a match, make a scratch,
No more candy store.

Mort couldn't blame Officer Potente for the crack about Jewish lightning. It was a well-known euphemism, even among Jews. As children, he and his friends had sung the "candy store" rhyme a thousand times in the schoolyard and when they played in the street.

The call with Potente had left Mort feeling even more shaken than before and now slightly desperate. He decided that another visit to 92 was warranted. This time he would be taken there by his hobbled vehicle. He didn't know what to expect, perhaps some insight on recent events, or just a sense of tranquility from seeing the house again. Merely imagining the sight that awaited him — the rock solid shell of the house he'd built — brought him a sense of ease. He remembered that on his last visit he'd seen that the place was gutted. The innards were being cleared by heavy machinery. The outer structure remained perfectly intact, a testament to how sturdy and well-designed the house was.

Descending from the summit lookout past the chalet at Beaver Lake and the police horse stables, Mort was continually distracted. One moment by the vacant tip of the Jag's hood, the next by rows of headstones behind the fence bordering Côte-des-Neiges cemetery, which spread out for miles over Mount-Royal's western slope. He almost missed veering right onto Decelles Avenue in front of the University of Montreal gate, a necessary turn to be able to make a left onto Queen Mary Road.

The Jag lumbered to a stop at the red light in front of Saint Joseph's Oratory on Queen Mary. Mort gazed up at the huge green-domed cathedral that sat atop the summit of Westmount like an enthroned monarch. Multi-million dollar homes lined the avenues behind the oratory like a throng of courtiers, while in front a hundred stairs cascaded down to a parking lot filled with cars and tourist buses.

Mort had always loved the Italianate granite-and-copper domed basilica, third largest of its kind in the world. It had been built by Brother Andre who, it was said, possessed the power to heal the sick. Brother Andre never lived to see the cathedral completed, but it stood as a permanent testament to the miracles he had performed and an enduring legacy of Quebec's deeply religious past.

Mort took Jackie and Rusty there often as kids. He told them stories about the infirm pilgrims who travelled from far and wide to climb the one hundred stairs on their knees to receive healing. Jackie and Rusty believed every word Mort told them about Brother Andre and his miracles. They didn't need much convincing, especially when they rode up the escalator inside the basilica — literally ascending to a higher plane — and arrived at the hushed, candle-lit chapel of Saint Joseph where they saw thousands of discarded wooden crutches and canes hanging from the walls.

The highlight of every trip to the oratory was seeing the embalmed heart of the faith healer encased in a glass reliquary. Brother Andre had requested that it be preserved and kept as protection for the oratory. Mort told Jackie and Rusty about how the heart had once been stolen. A $50,000 ransom demand was deemed to be a hoax, and, after missing for two years, the heart was mysteriously returned without the perpetrators ever being caught.

How many places in the world displayed such medieval oddities as a priest's embalmed heart? Mort had asked himself, proud to have even a small part of such shenanigans. In Communist Russia they displayed the mummified corpse of Vladimir Lenin at a mausoleum in Moscow's Red Square. The West was not immune to such gruesome reverence. Mort had heard that Einstein's brain had been preserved, and then sliced into pieces and shipped off to be studied at various universities in the United States and abroad.

Still, Brother Andre's pickled organ took the cake: sideshow gimmickry for the witless believing masses at its best, according to Mort. If nothing else, it alone was evidence that Montreal belonged to another continent and another century; an era of faith healers, miracle workers, magicians, carnival attractions, and freak shows. Mort wanted Jackie and Rusty to appreciate and delight in the whole story, just as he did. He wanted them to connect deeply and authentically to the city that claimed them. The oratory's crutches and canes and Brother Andre's embalmed heart were integral parts of that process, as were other favourite haunts, such as Belmont Park's Cyclone, Moshe Safdie's Habitat

67, and Buckminster Fuller's geodesic dome. Montreal was a city as bizarrely imagined as it was real, a place that had never lost its strange pedigree or appeal. Lately, it was the capital of festivals (jazz, comedy, movies, lobster), the birthplace of the Cirque du Soleil, a haven for video-game makers and pharmaceutical companies, the home of a spaceship-shaped Olympic Stadium, not to mention the first home of Major League Baseball in Canada. It was a mélange of cultures and styles; a Pandora's box of dissonant languages, voices, and rhythms; a hodgepodge of sensibilities, perspectives, and eras; a city of believers and of the faithful, whether Catholics who climbed stairs on their knees, Hasidic Jews, or Montreal Canadiens hockey fans. Above all, Montreal was a city that had won and lost, tried and failed, over and over again and somehow found its way. In a word, Montreal was home.

Mort drove down Queen Mary Road, a boulevard that tied Hampstead at one end to the slope of Mount Royal at the other like an umbilical cord. He crossed the Decarie Expressway, glancing two storeys down into its sunken hull to catch a glimpse of the vehicles zooming past underneath. The cavernous highway bisecting the island north-south was a wound, an epic gash that seemed like it might have been formed by prehistoric tectonic shifts, post–ice age glacial scarring, or maybe by Biblical decree from an angry god passing judgment against a sinful city. There was a moment in time, Mort remembered, when "Biblical" was the operative term.

On July 14, 1987, there was a flash flood. Four inches of rain fell on Montreal in less than two hours. The municipal sewage system throughout the city was overwhelmed. From under the pavement, water shot up like geysers, popping out steel manhole covers and turning them into deadly flying disks. Underpasses were flooded within minutes. Decarie filled up like a gigantic bathtub with over ten feet of water in sections. Hundreds of cars and buses stuck in afternoon rush-hour traffic sank like bath toys as the water rose. Mort remembered hearing the reports on the radio. His office staff ran back and forth yelling, "Have you heard what's happening? The island is sinking!" Mort remembered getting a panicked call from Mona.

"Come now, please Mort. You've got to come!" she pleaded. "The basement of the house is flooded! I don't know what to do!"

"There's nothing I can do," he said. "The whole damned city's flooded."

They'd been divorced for a year at that point, and Mort was still sore from losing the house in the settlement. He was tempted to go. Not for Mona's sake, but for the house's.

"The water's coming up the stairs. I'm scared it's going to reach the main floor," Mona begged.

Not rushing over to 92 was one of the hardest things Mort had ever done. Anyway, with so many roadways inundated, he would have probably gotten stranded if he'd tried.

"The water'll go down soon," Mort said to Mona in a doctor's detached voice. "Then you can call up the insurance. They'll send a clean-up crew."

Being indifferent to Mona on the phone, Mort reflected, may have been a mistake. It obviously hurt her. How else to explain what she did next?

In the days following the flood, Mort received a distressed phone call from Rusty. She said that her mother had gone bonkers, spending all day in the stinking, sewage-stained basement of the house making piles to discard. "Unsalvageable items," she called them. Mona was tossing out old clothes, winter jackets, shoes, and boots, and sporting goods, including skis, skates, hockey sticks, baseball bats and mitts, and tennis rackets.

But that wasn't all, she was trashing Mort's entire workshop of tools, including his table saw, his drill press, his workbench, all his screwdrivers, hammers, planes, and handsaws. How could she throw out hardware? Mort asked Rusty, outraged. Stainless-steel tools aren't damaged from water!

The worst of it, according to Rusty, was that Mona was trashing all the old family albums that were stored in the basement. Rusty broke down as she enumerated the album of family ski vacations at Squaw Valley and Heavenly Valley; the trip to Palm Springs; the Christmas vacations in Hallandale Beach at the Diplomat Hotel; the trip to Disney World in Orlando; the times they drove to Florida with stops in New York City, Washington, D.C., and Atlanta.

"All gone," Rusty said to Mort, audibly in tears. "All those photos albums, gone forever. I don't think Mom kept a single picture of us together. She even tossed out Jackie's Bar mitzvah album. And my sweet sixteen."

"They were unsalvageable," was Mona's emotionless response when Mort asked her why she'd trashed the photo albums. "Everything stunk of sewage. They were ruined, completely destroyed. The clothes were not even suitable for charitable donation."

"But the photos were in plastic sheets! Rusty said you threw out the negatives, too! How do you explain, trashing my tools?" Mort asked, incredulous.

"Unsalvageable," Mona repeated coldly.

Mort knew that what Mona really had in mind was to salvage her own life. She had taken advantage of an act of God to discard an unsalvageable past, wipe the slate clean by eradicating every documented trace of Mort's presence in her life and theirs together. It was a merciless operation, an amputation of the past, radical history-ectomy, cruellest to the only people who didn't have a say, but to whom the photo albums really mattered most: Jackie and Rusty.

Mort should have acted the hero. Had he gone the day of the flood he might have walked out with a photo album or two in his arms. It sat heavy on his heart that he hadn't taken them when he left the first time. Now only a few dozen pictures remained of Jackie and Rusty as kids. He had a couple of faded baby and toddler shots framed on his office desk, and a couple more passport-size shots crushed and folded away next to his loyalty, debit, and credit cards in his wallet.

Adding insult to injury, the remainder of Mona's library — the books that Mort hadn't managed to incinerate — had all been spared. Shortly after Mort left, Mona had moved them from the basement upstairs, filling shelves in the den and bedroom, her way of planting flags, claiming territory, declaring victory.

Cruising down Queen Mary past the town hall, Hampstead in late summer maintained the self-satisfied hues of genteel wealth. Tree-lined and flat, only in street designation did Hampstead recall its hilly, lush and more famous suburban London namesake. Past Dufferin, Finchley, Stratford, and curving toward Ellerdale, Mort began to feel that the houses of the "old" section exuded a certain nineteenth-century European charm with their brick facades covered in vine creepers and lawns dominated by thick, stately oaks and maples. Every time Mort crossed Ellerdale and entered the "newer" streets closer to Hampstead Park, he giggled inside with the thought that from its founding in 1914 by a cabal of Protestant bankers and industrialists, Hampstead had been as goyish as a restricted golf club, until the Jews started taking over in the late 1950s and early '60s. The municipality was now over 80 percent Jewish and annually competed with places like Forest Hill in Toronto as the wealthiest, most affluent community in Canada. The mayor had been Jewish for the last several decades, and from the late 1970s, Hampstead had an officially designated sister town in northern Israel. Stepsister would be more accurate since, except for its Jewish inhabitants, Hampstead had virtually nothing in common with Kiryat Shmona, which was regularly missile-bombed from southern Lebanon by Hezbollah terrorists.

Past the stop sign on Ellerdale, the Jag crossed Northcote and approached Merton, the last street before the left-hand turn onto Hampstead Road.

Mort had loved this garden-city suburb from the day he persuaded Mona's father Shimmy that buying a piece of undeveloped land on Hampstead Road was the best real-estate investment he could make. Shimmy was astute in business and didn't need much convincing. He saw that the Jews from Snowdon were headed down Queen Mary Road. He bought a double lot. Half was saved for Mort and Mona to build on, and the other half would be sold off for a tidy profit. The plan worked like a charm. Shimmy tripled his money in less than seven years.

Once the stone house with the one-of-a-kind fireplace was built and the family moved in, Mort dove headfirst into Hampstead life. When Jackie was old enough, he coached his son's Little League softball team in the summer and his hockey team in winter. Mort co-coached the Pee-Wee All-Star hockey team, too, and organized Hampstead's first-ever international all-star hockey series between Hampstead and Englewood, New Jersey. He got the idea from the Canada-Russia Series. He booked a bus, found homes to billet the players, and twisted the arms of the Hampstead town council to buy the kids new uniforms that would make the town proud of their "Pee-Wee hockey ambassadors": bright orange sweaters with a "Hampstead Hockey" crest in the middle and matching orange-and-white striped hockey socks. At first, the council balked at the idea. They didn't have a budget, Mort was told at a town meeting. Pointing his finger at Hampstead's first-ever Jewish mayor, a lawyer named Izzy Shifsky, Mort stood up and said, "Don't tell me you want our kids to go down to New Jersey looking like schleppers?" The mayor and his predominantly Jewish council relented, voting unanimously to approve the expenditure for new uniforms and bus rental, but the coaches and adult chaperones would have to pay for their own hotel accommodations in New Jersey.

At the time, Hampstead Park had a modest recreation hut, a dozen clay tennis courts, some basketball nets, and a wading pool. The softball diamonds were kept in acceptable condition. There were four backstops, one at each corner of a large square field facing the middle, which meant that the centre fields of all four baseball diamonds overlapped liked a Venn diagram. The Hampstead Pee-Wee softballers generally couldn't hit the ball far enough to create a player collision in the centre, but the possibility was there, and well-hit balls regularly rolled into the outfields of other games in progress.

The greatest shame of Hampstead recreation, though, was that the town did not have an indoor skating rink. In winter, wooden boards were erected on the basketball courts to form an outdoor rink. Weekday evenings, Atom, Mosquito, Pee-Wee, and Midget leagues played there. Regular practices for all four leagues were also scheduled, as well as free skates. Every day at midnight, the rink was shovelled and manually watered by the recreation staff with garden hoses. In spite of all the effort, the ice surface remained choppy, uneven, and slow. By mid-season it was virtually unplayable, which didn't really matter since any enjoyment that existed from playing outside in the fresh air during the months of December and January had already evaporated by early February when it was 20 degrees below zero.

Mort was behind the bench coaching house league one frigid February night, bouncing up and down on his toes trying to stay warm. He watched the Pee-Wees chug up and down the rink, huffing and puffing thick vapours through their plastic mouthguards as they slapped at the stuttering, rolling puck and tripped on inch-deep ice ruts. He asked himself, why should our kids freeze their asses off outside like this? There were comfortable indoor rinks with clean, soft ice and Zamboni machines in Notre-Dame-de-Grâce and Montreal West. Why couldn't Hampstead have one, too? A rich town like Hampstead, for Chrissakes! It didn't make sense. "It's time that our kids got their own indoor rink," he said to himself. This was the beginning of Mort's full-fledged immersion into municipal politics.

A plan of action began to take shape when a fellow hockey parent mentioned that the Heather Curling Club on Cleve Road in Hampstead was going bankrupt. He didn't doubt the reports of the club's imminent demise since it was well-known that Jews weren't big curlers. He called the club's president, a fellow named Beery, to confirm and asked if he could tour the facility with another hockey parent who was an engineer. Together they would explore the possibility of modifying the curling sheets into a hockey surface.

The technicalities checked out. It was possible, and, relatively speaking, not that expensive. The existing refrigeration system could be expanded to cover hockey dimensions. Another crucial piece of information was uncovered by Mort during the course of his investigations. The Town of Hampstead held the mortgage on the property. The fate of the club rested in the hands of the mayor and his council. The mayor had been keeping the club's bankruptcy quiet. Mort knew that he would inevitably have to face the council once more.

Even before Mort learned that the city planned to foreclose on the club's mortgage and sell off the building to the highest bidder, he began recruiting hockey families to his cause. When he sensed his support was firm, he invited several dozen parents to accompany him to a council meeting. It was a surprise attack on town officials. The hockey parents filled the small meeting room and Mort, acting as their spokesman, raised the issue of the curling club and presented the engineer's report to show that they meant business.

Mort was already well aware that Mayor Shifsky and his councilmen considered him a shit-disturber. But the hostile response he received from them was entirely unexpected. Shifsky did everything possible to bury the engineer's report and stonewall Mort's attempts to raise the matter again in council. There were powerful interests operating behind the scenes, Mort figured. Suddenly, news broke that the town planned to use funds from the sale of the curling club to buy new snow-removal equipment. It was Shifsky's end-run around the indoor rink proposal.

The game was on. Mort knew that if he didn't do something drastic and fast, his side would lose. His next move had to be radical. He decided that he would leverage his public support to force a referendum on the issue. Let the citizens decide whether they wanted their children to have an indoor hockey arena or new snowplows.

It is true that the Hampstead referendum of 1975 has since been overshadowed in the annals of Quebec politics by two other referenda, in 1980 and 1996, on whether the province should remain a part of Canada or separate as an independent country. But the fact remains that the referendum forced by Mort Halbman pitting snow-removal equipment against an indoor rink came first.

Collecting the requisite number of signatures wasn't difficult. It was the task of organizing and funding a full-scale campaign that Mort worried about. They may have lacked the resources and endorsement of town officials, but Mort knew that his cause had something infinitely more valuable: kids who wanted to play hockey. He gathered groups of Atom, Mosquito, and Pee-Wee players to dress up in their Hampstead house-league sweaters and go door to door with their parents, distributing flyers.

At first the campaign went well. Across Fleet Road in the newer sections of town, along Belsize, Netherwood, Holly, Applewood, Colchester, Fallbrook, and Harrow, where young families had built sprawling homes in the last ten years, their message was welcomed.

Articles soon began to appear in the local weekly, *The Hampsteader*, citing the age of the town's snow-removal equipment and projecting the long-term costs of maintaining and repairing the rusting machinery. More articles spoke of the exorbitant annual cost of maintaining a new indoor arena. A rumour began circulating that the sale of the curling club was needed to stave off a shortfall of the municipal budget and that if it didn't pass, property taxes would increase significantly.

Even before the referendum was officially called, the mayor's posters had started appearing. Overnight, signs that said, "YES, Hampstead Deserves Clean Streets!" were posted along Queen Mary Road, going through the centre of town from City Hall all the way down to Fleet.

The hockey parents responded by putting handmade posters on the same poles above the mayor's posters, saying "YES, Our Kids Need a Safe Place to Play."

Then the mayor put up more posters that said, "YES, the Time is NOW to Invest in Our Town's Future!" And the parents volleyed back by putting up more posters that said, "YES, Our Kids Deserve Better!"

A curious and unprecedented situation arose. With neither of the referendum sides wanting to seem like the negative position, the traditional Yes versus No model was inadvertently chucked out the window. Both parties tried to sell themselves as the positive alternative. It was yes against yes.

The mayor erected signs saying, "A YES Vote Means a Better Quality of Life for All Citizens!"

And the parents responded by plastering up posters that said, "YES, Our Kids' Future is OUR Future!"

Quebec politics would never see another campaign like it. The Hampstead referendum was pandemonium. There were posters on top of posters on top of posters, covering every square inch of public space, every telephone pole, mailbox, fire hydrant, public bench, bus stop, and tree trunk thick enough to hold them. Well-mannered, well-coiffed Hampstead, a town where clotheslines were made illegal for their unsightliness, looked positively hippy, like a rag-tag, patchwork vagabond from a Bob Dylan song. The citizens were thoroughly confused by all the messages. They hadn't the slightest clue what they were voting for, or against, or even whether there *was* anything to vote against.

Needless to say, it didn't take a week after the referendum was over for the town council to pass a law limiting the number of posters allowed during elections and restricting the height and location where they could appear on public property.

Mort and his boys remained optimistic until they began canvassing in the older sections of town. Door-knocking along Thurlow, Stratford, Granville, Dufferin, and MacDonald, it became clear that the church-going retirees who feared icy sidewalks and broken hips were almost unanimously in favour of new snow-removal equipment.

The vote wasn't even close. Snowplows won out. That and voter apathy. Child-rearing parents stayed home on voting night and retirees came out in droves.

A fleet of shiny new snowplows and snow blowers were bought. Hampstead's streets would forevermore be kept spotless in winter, except during municipal strikes, which happened every few years. Property taxes skyrocketed in spite of what the mayor had said during the referendum. Shifsky won four consecutive terms despite Mort never voting for him once.

Mort didn't chastise himself for being naive about municipal politics. He was proud of what he'd done. His heart had been in the right place — with the kids. Hampstead would never build its own indoor arena. And, as far as Mort was concerned, it didn't deserve one, anyway.

* * *

The Jag cruised past Merton and came to the stop sign on Hampstead Road. Mort glanced over at Hampstead Park on his right. New trees had been planted and a running track circling the park had recently been built. The baseball backstops had been replaced and the recreation chalet had undergone a facelift to accommodate the construction of a brand-new Olympic-size swimming pool.

Mort turned the steering wheel and loosened his grip to let it rewind. Facing the bottom of Hampstead Road, he thought he was seeing a mirage in reverse; the vaporous desert vision of an oasis that was there in reality, but appeared at a hallucinogenic distance to be missing. The closer Mort got, the more real the vision became.

92 Hampstead Road *was* gone. The house, the stone walls, the fireplace, everything gone. Vanished. Swept away. Stolen in a cloud of dust.

nine

"Where've you been?"

"Around."

"I've been looking for you. Didn't you get the message I left yesterday?"

"Yeah." Mort didn't feel like talking.

He wasn't sure why he'd bothered to answer his cell. Sitting alone in the corner booth at Snowdon Deli, he was still shaken up by what he'd seen on Hampstead Road, or rather what he hadn't seen.

The Jag had rolled past the empty lot without stopping. Mort had stared out through the passenger side window. He hadn't reached the neighbour's house when his mind went blank — in an instant becoming as vacant as the lot he'd just passed — and from that point on his vehicle was driving on autopilot. It U-turned and headed back in the direction of the expressway.

The stoplight at Van Horne and Decarie was red. The vehicle waited, vibrating and agitated. When the light turned green, the Jag turned right and proceeded cautiously along the Decarie service road. Mort's gaze followed the edge of the security railing above the expressway. He thought of the cliff-like drop on the other side. It was a precipice, a channel that could be crossed, *needed* to be crossed. Although the day was young and the sun was shining bright in a cloudless azure sky, Mort felt the need to seek shelter.

His irreplaceable house was gone. He'd tried to prepare himself, but now that it was a reality he could hardly believe it. The house built entirely from Mount-Royal stone. It was practically a tourist attraction. Folks would purposely drive by the corner of Hampstead and Minden just to see it. Residents took their bearings from the house. They'd give directions saying, "Around the corner from the stone house with the basketball net in the driveway." Or "Go down the street with the big stone house." There wasn't another house like it, nor was there likely to ever be one.

Mort didn't feel like talking or eating, but nevertheless instinctively headed for the Snowdon Deli, where the long brightly lit glass display cases adorned with platters of knishes, smoked meat, *kneydlach*, and chopped liver, would provide a sense of comfort.

Watching the stream of customers picking up pre-ordered boxes of party sandwiches, and hearing the friendly banter of the aproned servers — Manny, Jimmy, and Morry, who'd worked together behind the counter for more than thirty years — soothed his nerves. *Some things do last*, Mort thought to himself. Before sitting down, he'd already decided to leave a hefty tip for the waitress whether he ate or not. A show of appreciation for the place and all the Sundays he'd spent there. He ordered a coffee just so the waitress wouldn't think he was a *schnorrer*. While he waited for his coffee, his cellphone rang. The caller ID identified Gerstein. Mort sighed and answered. "Listen, Mickey, can I call you back?" he said, barely giving Gerstein a chance to say hello.

"What's the matter? You sound like crap."

"Nothing. I just don't feel like talking. That's all."

"It's about my sister, Sandy —" Gerstein continued, ignoring Mort's request.

"It's not the right time. Look, I was going to call you back about Sandy. It's nothing personal against your sister —"

"She's not looking for some good-time Charlie or sugar daddy. She's a tough cookie and can take care of herself. I just thought you'd be good company for her. You know, take her out for dinner. Try it just once. It'd do you some good. Have I ever steered you wrong?" Gerstein asked, knowing what Mort would say next.

"Wonderful Wheeling, West Virginia," Mort answered on cue.

"Well, that didn't end so badly, did it?" Gerstein shot back rhetorically.

"No, only jobless in California for two months then back home with our tails between our legs you *schmuckalufski*," Mort smiled into the phone, the fog of futility beginning to lift, his bearings slowly returning thanks to his oldest buddy.

"As I recall you were good company for the broad upstairs. Isn't that what she said: *'good company.'* Anyway, Sandy's not looking for more."

Mort and Gerstein had gone back to the Wheeling mansion, packed their bags as fast as they could, and headed straight to the bus station in town. They made no effort to find their host to thank him for the accommodations. They figured that getting out of town as quickly as was humanly possible was all the gratitude the mystery man needed after the way they'd underbet at the racetrack. Their measly winnings, minus the hundred dollars they'd tipped the woman, were enough to buy a pair of tickets for the two-day bus ride across the continent to Hollywood. They'd probably have sufficient money left over to cover room and board for a month or two. First they'd soak up the sights for a few days and then find jobs.

On the bus, they met a fellow who seemed about their age and claimed to be from Beverly Hills. His father was in the theatre business. He promised a ride from his dad, who was picking him up at the bus station, and recommended lodging a few blocks from Hollywood Boulevard where Mort and Gerstein could rent cheaply.

The apartment building looked decent: stucco painted robin's egg blue with red-and-white candy-striped awnings over the windows. The owners were an elderly Jewish couple originally from the Bronx. They took an instant liking to the boys from Montreal. Mort and Gerstein were assigned a ground-floor studio apartment that came furnished with a kitchenette, a mini-fridge, and hot plate, and a Murphy bed that flipped up into the wall. "It's one of our better rooms," Ida Nadel, the landlady told them.

"A little advice. Stay away from the people upstairs," Ida's husband Ralph warned. "They're not for nice Jewish boys like you."

Mort soon found out why the ground-floor room was one of the *better* rooms and not one of the *best* ones. The building's phone was located in the hallway outside their door. Sleep-deprived from the long, cramped bus ride from Wheeling, the boys were hoping to get some extra shut-eye. The incessant phone ringing outside their door at all hours of the night rendered that impossible.

Early Sunday morning, Gerstein groggily dragged himself out of bed and was cooking bacon and eggs on the hot plate when the hallway phone rang. Footsteps came clacking down the stairs and then a shrill voice was heard answering above the sizzle of bacon. Shortly afterward came a rude pounding on their door. Spatula-armed Gerstein leaped to open it.

"What d'ya think you're doin'?"

"Excuse me?"

"Stinkin' up the whole joint like that!"

"We're making breakfast." The obvious was all Gerstein was capable of muttering in the presence of the platinum-blond Diana Dors lookalike in pedal pushers and a halter top who filled the doorway.

"Yeah, I can see that," she said, scrunching up her button nose. "Smell it, too. Me and my girl would appreciate if you could put a lid on it."

"Sure thing," Gerstein said, lowering his spatula.

"Tell you what. Since you seem so agreeable, and are apparently domestically inclined," the bombshell said winking in the direction of Gerstein's spatula, "why don't you come upstairs and I'll give you some disinfectant spray to cover up the stench."

Gerstein dumped the utensil and followed the blonde out the door. Mort hesitated, thinking about Ralph Nadel's warning, then instantly banished it from his mind. Like Gerstein, he couldn't wait to get upstairs.

"Name's Celine, and this here is Angelina, the blonde said, as her apartment door swung open revealing a scarlet-haired stunner in flared shorts and a bowling shirt, who appeared to be in the middle of doing calisthenics, legs spread, arms raised in Y formation. Glenn Miller's "Moonlight Serenade" played on an unseen phonograph in the background. Slender, with high cheekbones, she was a dead ringer for Maureen O'Hara and ignored Mort and Gerstein as they inched into the room.

Mort elbowed Gerstein. "Do all the women in this town resemble movie stars?"

"Where'd you say you was from?" Celine asked, ducking into a living room closet, her voice rising to be heard.

"We didn't say," Gerstein said.

"I just figured. Everyone in this town is from somewhere else, isn't that right, Angie?"

"Montreal," Mort piped up. "I'm Mort, and this here's Mickey."

"All the way from Canada? No kidding. We met some Canadian boys once, didn't we Angie? From Toronto, I think."

Angelina bent and stretched her body alphabetically without paying any attention to the conversation. The boys couldn't take their eyes off her but she didn't seem to care, as if being stared at was normal.

Celine emerged from the closet and crossed the room, holding out a spray bottle like she was offering a gift. As she approached, Mort noticed the apartment walls for the first time. Unframed black-and-white images of shadowy figures were haphazardly tacked up everywhere. Mort took a step into the room to get a better look. They were pin-up pictures, women in languid poses, some partially clothed and others completely nude. Mixed in with the pin-up shots were photographs of ladies dolled up in hats and cocktail dresses, accompanied by various men, either walking on the street arm in arm, eating in restaurants, or seated in cars. Some images were blurry while others were sharply focused. It wasn't until Mort recognized Celine and Angelina in the photos with the different men that he realized the pin-up shots, the nudies, were them, too.

"Here, this'll take away the smell," Celine said, handing the spray bottle to Mort. "It'd be nice to see you boys again sometime soon. Don't you think so, Angie? Did you hear? These boys are from Montreal."

"Sure thing," Mort said, hugging the bottle to his chest. "We'll return this as soon as the smell's cleared."

"And while you're at it, why doncha open a window?" Angelina finally said, her head swinging upside down between her spread legs.

"D'you think they're hookers?" Mort asked Gerstein when they were back downstairs in their apartment.

"Might be," Gerstein answered hopefully.

"Since when do hookers take pictures of themselves?"

"I don't know," Gerstein said. "Maybe it's something new to the trade. You know, like souvenirs that the johns can take home with them."

"You think we should stay away from them?" Mort asked.

"What for? They seem like ordinary girls," Gerstein said, knowing full well that there was nothing *ordinary* about them. "This is Hollywood Morty. Forget Montreal. Forget the Fairmount High girls. Forget Malca Lichtman who didn't know a hand job from a nose job, or Rivky Zlotnick who thought stroking balls was what her old man did on the golf course. If you're going to have a shot at making it in LA you better learn to loosen up and go with the flow."

Going with the flow was exactly what Mort and Gerstein did. Celine and Angelina were as friendly and nice as two ordinary girls could be. Over the next few days they were the perfect tour guides, showing Mort and Gerstein all the sights in and around Hollywood. They went to Grauman's Chinese Theatre to see the handprints of the movie stars in the concrete, drove through Beverly Hills to gawk at the mansions, rode the carousel at the Santa Monica Pier, and cruised along Mulholland Drive at night to view the lights of Hollywood shimmering like a handful of gems in the velvet pocket of the San Fernando Valley. No matter where they went, the restaurants, the theatres, or the amusement park, the girls paid for everything. Not once did they ask Mort or Gerstein for a dime. Feeling uncomfortable, the boys offered to pay, but the girls steadfastly refused, with Celine saying, "This is our treat. You're guests in our town. When we come to Montreal, then you can take us out." Under the circumstances, Mort was okay with the arrangement. If not for the girls treating them they would have run out of money fast, and anyway, the girls seemed to possess an endless supply of cash.

"If they're hookers," Mort whispered to Gerstein, "they're not very good at it. I mean they're paying *us* to be with *them*."

"You're good company," Celine said to Mort, as they strolled along the boardwalk after an afternoon at the beach, her arm looped through his. "Polite. Real gentlemen. None of the hanky-panky stuff. Me and my girl like that."

Their first two weeks in Hollywood could not have been more perfect if it had been scripted: a great apartment close to Hollywood Boulevard, two beautiful women to show them around town, and everything paid for. The only annoyance was the phone ringing at strange hours, always for the girls, who would then quietly retreat into their apartment upstairs and disappear for long stretches of time.

This gave Mort and Gerstein time to look for jobs. They answered the Want ads in the paper and quickly discovered that they were not the only back-Easters who'd decided to seek their fortune in sunny California. The lines stretched around the block at the car dealerships and department stores who'd advertised for salesmen, and at restaurants seeking waiters.

"There's no way I'm selling vacuum cleaners door to door," Gerstein said to Mort, who was looking at a Hoover ad in the classifieds. "Peddling door to door I can do in Montreal where I know the route off by heart."

Several weeks of job hunting in vain began to take its toll. Mort and Gerstein knew that they were missing the key ingredient for success, the one thing that would give them a leg-up over all the other unemployed *schmoes*, something they had in abundance back home: connections. The only connections they'd made in Hollywood, Celine and Angelina, never talked about their work or who they knew. Not once did they offer to help the boys find jobs. Actually, they studiously avoided the subject, as if they didn't want the boys to find employment.

Mort and Gerstein were standing in yet another line together with a hundred other job applicants outside a department store on Ventura Boulevard, when a Studebaker pulled up a few yards away beside the curb. Mort immediately recognized Celine in the passenger seat. Her window was down and she was with a man. Mort called out to her and waved. She looked directly at him stone-faced, turned her head away, and rolled up her window.

Mort was sure Celine had seen him. He wanted to sort out what was going on, ask her if she was in some kind of trouble. As he left the line to approach the car, it sped away.

"Maybe she didn't recognize you," Gerstein said.

"She saw me plain as day. It was like she didn't *want* to recognize me."

"Don't let it get to you," Gerstein said.

Mort couldn't help letting it get to him.

A few evenings later, Celine and Angelina took Mort and Gerstein up to the Griffith Observatory for a planetarium show. They sat boy, girl, boy, girl, heads angled up to face the curved underside of the dome. The lights slowly dimmed and the room became blacker than any night Mort had ever seen from atop Mount-Royal. Tiny specks of light emerged like glistening bubbles rising in Coca-Cola. The moon floated into view, and then planets appeared, greenish Venus and reddish Mars. Celine said, "Jeez, don't it almost make you believe in God?" her forearm lightly brushing against Mort's on their shared armrest. Her fingers crawled into his half-closed fist like a small fragile creature seeking cover. Mort enjoyed the physical contact between them, not that he would ever dare to initiate it. Their interaction, he knew, could never go any further. Flirtation between them was more akin to children playing than adult behaviour. He sensed that lurking in the background, keeping Celine at a safe distance, there was a dark force, like the force that kept the moon orbiting and not letting it crash down to earth. She belonged to someone else, she was another's property, and the time she spent with Mort, was borrowed.

"Can I ask you something?" Mort whispered into Celine's ear, their heads tilted up, both sets of eyes fixed at the night sky projected on the concave underside of the planetarium roof.

"Sure."

"About the pictures on your walls. And the phone calls. And that day on Ventura Boulevard … I know that you saw me."

"It's nothing."

"Look, you've been swell with me and Gerstein. I don't mean to pry."

"Please, don't … just drop it, okay?" Celine became agitated.

"It's just that —" Mort hesitated, sensing that he'd already crossed a line.

"Never mind," she interrupted. The conversation ended abruptly with Celine slipping her hand out of Mort's.

Celine and Angelina were not seen again for over a week. When the phone rang, one of the girls came downstairs, answered it, and returned back upstairs without so much as a friendly knock on their door.

Seemingly overnight, Mort's and Gerstein's Hollywood escapade was turning into a bust. The boys couldn't find jobs and their money was running out fast. Mort received a message from his older brother Hymie in Montreal that their mother was ill and she wanted him to come home. Mort knew that the way things were going, they wouldn't be able to sustain themselves in California for much longer, anyway. He couldn't leave without getting some answers. He decided on an ambush. The night before departing he waited up past midnight. As expected, the phone rang. Hearing the familiar voice in the hallway answering, "Hello," he swung his apartment door open.

Celine was dressed to the nines in pumps, lace stockings, and a cocktail dress, heading out for a late night on the town with a new suitor. Mort felt a sharp pang of jealousy.

"Hi."

Celine hung up the phone. She looked at Mort blankly.

"Why'd you dump us?"

"You wouldn't understand," she said, looking away.

"My buddy and I have decided to leave."

"I figured."

"Before we leave I need to know. Please."

"It was nice. You and your friend were good company. Me and my girl liked you. Then you had to go and ruin it."

"Ruin it?! You think *we* ruined it? What are you talking about?! You were the ones who dumped *us!*"

"You wouldn't play along, is all."

"Play along? Play along with what?"

"We thought you boys would be different. You're all the same. I know what you're thinking about me and Angie. Well, you're wrong. It's not like that at all."

"Thinking what? We weren't thinking anything."

"Oh sure you were. That night at the planetarium. The moon and the stars. It was all very romantic. Then you started asking questions. You had to know. Well, I'll tell you what you want to know. That day on Ventura, sure, I saw you. I was working."

"You were in a car with a man. What kind of work is that? Or do I really need to ask."

"It was an agency job."

"What does that mean? What's an agency job?"

"Angie and I, we help women in trouble."

"What sort of trouble?"

"Man trouble. We help them prove that their husbands are two-timing low-lifes. So they can divorce them."

"The pictures on your walls —"

"We came to Hollywood to be in pictures. What else do you expect? We act for the cameras, just not movie cameras. We go out with the men. Have some laughs. Then the women see the men they married for the scum they really are. You know, it's really too bad about you, Mort. We were having such a nice time together. You were good company," Celine repeated, gently stroking Mort's cheek with a gloved finger. "Too bad you couldn't stick to the script."

"The script? What script?" Mort blushed.

"The script that says play your role and don't ask questions. Remember, this is Hollywood, hon."

Los Angeles had been a fiasco, worse than Wheeling, West Virginia. Mort and Gerstein hardly spoke on the bus ride from Los Angeles to Chicago, and only sporadically from Chicago to Montreal. Mort's brother had wired him enough money to cover the balance of owed rent, some food, and fare home. Mort was humiliated, and the only greater embarrassment was having his family bail him out. He was returning home an abject failure and was taking it hard. Gerstein, on the other hand, seemed relatively unaffected. He enjoyed the trip and had continuous conversations with the turnover of passengers who embarked and disembarked between stops. He smiled at the passing landscape and remarked stupidly on every cornfield, silo, and cow — at least it seemed that way to Mort.

"You know something," Mort finally said. "You're a goddamn imbecile. We left Montreal in the early morning dark, made our great escape to find jobs, make a fresh start in California. Now look at us. We're going home with empty pockets and nothing to show for our efforts. Damn it, Gerstein! Doesn't it make a whiff of difference to you that we had to get rescued by family? Do you know what they must be saying about us right now? Aren't you the least bit ashamed?"

"Ashamed? For what? We met some nice people. Experienced some new things. Had some good times. You know what your problem is, Halbman? You expect too much. And when things don't measure up to your expectations, you're disappointed and humiliated. We started fresh once. So now we're starting fresh again. For us, Montreal will never be the same."

Thinking about California fifty years later, Mort had to admit that Gerstein may have been right about his expectations — the meshuganner wasn't such an imbecile, after all. They had enjoyed a good time while it lasted. And Montreal definitely wasn't the same afterward.

When Mort got home, he went straight to work. He had decided on the bus ride — somewhere between Lansing and Detroit, Michigan — that from then on he would earn the respect of his family and peers. He took a job with Hymie in the garment business. He started by sweeping the factory floor and, step by step, learned all the departments, from shipping and receiving, to laying up goods and cutting, to sewing, and finally pattern-making and designing. In a few years he was out on the road selling to boutiques. It didn't take long to break into the major department stores, The Hudson's Bay Company, Simpsons, and Sears Roebuck. The family business grew at a steady rate. Mort helped his mother out at home with expenses and filled his personal bank account with whatever was left over.

In 1960, he married Mona, Shimmy Solomon's daughter, the king of Canadian dress manufacturers. Did that make him *schmatta* royalty? He certainly felt that it did. Mona gave him two beautiful heirs and he built his Hampstead palace. His life was going swimmingly. Everything was falling into place. And then, imperceptibly, it all started to unravel. Almost fifty years later, he still couldn't say exactly how or when or why.

Mort's mind was in overdrive, sifting through memories, re-ordering events without logic, a jumble of meanings and feelings. One moment he was in the Snowdon Deli on Decarie, and the next he was in Hollywood having his heart broken for the first time by an "agency girl."

He stared into his coffee, his fingers locked around the mug as if he were gripping the rim of a murky hole that threatened to suck him down. He felt light, unanchored, helpless.

ten

Being on the east side of Decarie, the mountain side as opposed to the newer Hampstead side, somehow felt safer to Mort.

From Snowdon Deli he drove north along the expressway service road, past Svetlana Coiffure, Librarie Russe, another store selling Russian souvenirs and trinkets, and two drugstores, Weinberg's and Greenbaums's.

In the distance, near Decarie's north end, Mort could make out the giant three-storey, forty-foot-diameter, fibreglass-reinforced plastic sphere that was Gibeau Orange Julep. Through the haze of car fumes rising out of the cavernous expressway like volcanic gas escaping from a crack in the earth, the drive-in's luminous orange dome appeared like a spaceship just landed. When they were kids, Mort used to take Jackie and Rusty to Orange Julep for hot dogs, french fries, and a pint of their famously irresistible frothy orange beverage. Rumour was that the drink owed its considerable addictiveness to whipped egg whites blended with a fiercely guarded formula of spices that you wouldn't think belonged in a fruit beverage of any sort and would elicit vomitous gagging were it known.

Orange Julep had been a magnet for two generations. The day the *ouvert* sign went up on Decarie was the first genuinely reliable indication that winter was finally over and summer was speeding in full-throttle. The new season's first pint of julep was a rite of spring for Montrealers and the drive-in was *the* place to see and be seen. Teenagers who'd recently earned their driver's licences would celebrate by ceremoniously taking Dad's car there as a demonstration of hard-won independence. All summer long, souped-up convertibles and muscle cars were parked around the huge orange globe in semicircular rows five deep, hoods pointing to the front like parishioners oriented toward a pulpit. On their pilgrimages, Mort would describe to Jackie and Rusty how, not so many years ago, there were roller-skating waitresses clad in shorts and thick money pouches that sagged from their belt loops who would take your order and deliver the food on trays directly to your car window.

The waitresses on wheels may have gone, but that didn't diminish the experience for Jackie. On the contrary, he sensed that here was a place with a history. Jackie couldn't wait to stand in line with Mort at the counter while Rusty waited in the car. He would ask his father to lift him up by the armpits so he could watch the julep-making machine through the Plexiglas window behind the counter. He would stare at the huge, crushing contraption made of gears, levers, and plastic tubes as it swallowed hopper after hopper of oranges whole with skin, and seeds at one end, and squeezed out the delectable elixir from the other. The mechanical spectacle enhanced Jackie's already entrenched feeling that Gibeau Orange Julep was utterly cloaked in mythology and mystery. He wondered about what went on in the sealed upper reaches of the giant orange globe. Did people live or work up there? Obviously, whatever went on, it had to be important; covert operations, he told his father. Probably, there was some sort of command centre with television screens and antennas manned by military types, colonels and three-star generals who communicated with satellites that spied on the Russians, tracked arms shipments and missile installations. In Jackie's ten-year-old mind he knew that somewhere deep in the Orange Julep's core there was a red phone, a hotline direct to the Pentagon, maybe even to the White House.

At Côte-Sainte-Catherine Road, Mort turned right. He crossed the streets of Trans Island, Mountain Sights, and rolled up to the stoplight on Westbury Avenue, coming to a halt between two modern structures with darkly tinted windows that faced each other on either side of the street. On his left was Cummings House, and to his right the Saidye Bronfman Centre for the Arts. Vertical banners hung from lampposts along Côte-Sainte-Catherine designating the block "The Jewish Community Campus."

The area was a curious mix; two stoic, modern glass edifices, the shorter one a cultural centre and the other, the central bureaucracy of the official Jewish community, Montreal's Duma. The surrounding streets were lined with flat-roofed, attached upper and lower postwar duplexes, many occupied by Jewish society's bottom-rung, newly arrived immigrants from the former Soviet Union, Orthodox Jewish families with rapidly multiplying broods, and Yiddish-speaking retirees scraping by on paltry garment union pensions. They inhabited this area because of the low rents, and to be close to the array of community-funded social services: the Immigrant Aid Society, the Jewish Public Library, the YM-YWHA Ben Weider Jewish Community Centre, and the Hebrew day schools. The Golden Age Association was around the corner on Westbury, offering bridge games, book reviews, lectures on breast and prostate health, knitting and birdhouse-making workshops, and a cafeteria that served tasty bowls of subsidized borscht. A short block away was Bronfman House, an assisted-living residence that had a two-year waiting list to get an apartment.

Out of the corner of his eye, Mort glimpsed the giant severed head of a bull with horns assembled from chunks of stone plunked down on the entrance steps of the Saidye Bronfman Centre. "No doubt this eyesore is meant to be art," Mort muttered disparagingly, a symbol of sacrifice or the sin of the biblical Golden Calf. Behind the sculpture, draped over the building's immense panels of black glass, were broad, extravagantly lettered posters publicizing upcoming theatrical performances. One had a sepia-coloured image of a half-naked man stooped and wrapped in leg irons and heavy chains, a heart-shaped iron padlock dangling from his neck like a millstone keepsake. The signage announced an original musical play based on the life of Harry Houdini performed in Yiddish *with English and French subtitles*. Since when did plays come with subtitles? No, the word was *surtitles*, whatever that was.

Here, in a nutshell, in the span of a few short blocks, were Mort's annual donations to Combined Jewish Appeal hard at work keeping the Jewish flame burning. A mishmash of old and new: Yiddish plays translated in English and French; young Russian refugees who opened magazine stores and beauty shops as a way of trying to forget the misery they'd fled; and old Jewish pensioners living in subsidized-housing, consuming subsidized soup who had little to hold on to *but* their memories. Mort could imagine that the two groups, the Russian exiles and the Yiddish pensioners, understood one other better than he could understand either.

This neighbourhood, only a few blocks across the Decarie Expressway, was as far away from Hampstead as a separate continent. Mort knew little about it, except that it was where he mailed his cheques every September when the call for donations came, and where judicious professionals, after skimming a self-sustaining (yet reasonable) tithe off the top, presumably put his money to good use helping brethren in need.

Traversing Westbury, the Jag rolled up Côte-Sainte-Catherine past Mackenzie King Park and stopped at the traffic light on Victoria Avenue. A group of skinny, dark-skinned Asian youth congregated in the entranceway of the Metro station on the opposite corner of the street. They laughed, shoved one another, milled about, and periodically went into the Metro station as if waiting impatiently for someone special to emerge from out of the windy underground tunnel. Next door to the Metro was Marché Kim-Po, a Korean-owned grocery store, and directly across was another grocery store, The New World, this one specializing in Asian fruits and vegetables. Victoria Avenue was lined with a host of Vietnamese, Thai, and Filipino restaurants, beauty shops, and, facing the Metro entrance, the offices of a driving school called École de conduite Hope. Mort remembered seeing sub-compacts with signs on their roofs that said *Hope* circulating through the streets of Snowdon with student drivers at the steering wheels, usually Asians, Indians, or Africans. Now he knew where the *Hope* cars originated.

Mort proceeded up Côte-Sainte-Catherine toward Côte-des-Neiges, the next major cross-street. He could sense the gradual slope of Mount-Royal begin to take hold as the car demanded increased pressure from his accelerator foot. The haphazard conglomeration of architecturally mixed-era structures that constituted the Jewish General Hospital came into full view at Lajoie Avenue.

Mort donated annually to the Jewish General, separately from his yearly gift to Combined Jewish Appeal. He gave the hospital the exact same amount as he gave to Combined Jewish Appeal, equally splitting the sum his accountant determined to be the money he would otherwise have to pay to the government in income taxes. There were years when dress sales were good and the sums given to both organizations were considerable. Other years, sales were down and the charities felt the pinch, too. Mort considered every penny out of his pocket donated to the Jewish General Hospital as an investment in his future. He knew that one way or another he would end up there, suffering from heart-disease or late-stage cancer, products of a careless, undisciplined life. He'd actually been relatively healthy up to this point, something that he considered pure luck. The hospital's services had only been required a few times, the last being a routine colonoscopy, which had been performed by a young, impeccably-groomed, disconcertingly tanned, and dapper Doctor Cohen. Mort remembered the doctor's appearance in particular because it seemed so utterly incongruous with the procedure he performed day in and day out. While the snake-head video camera was making its way into Mort's lubricated rectum to document the inside of his intestines, he told Doctor Cohen — he'd refused general anesthesia and was wide awake for the whole show — that he'd been a generous supporter of the Jewish hospital for years. "Maybe it'll buy me a clear test," he said with an uncomfortable chuckle.

"Let's hope so," the doctor replied from behind Mort, shoving the tube farther up his ass. When the results came back negative, Mort's first thought was to celebrate by going to Snowdon Deli for a baseball-sized scoop of chopped liver with onions. The colonoscopy had proven that the dish was medically harmless.

Waiting for the light to change on Lajoie, Mort spied a slim, familiar figure waiting between two parked cars for an opening in the traffic to jaywalk. The long, grey ponytail that flapped side to side made Gordon Ash so conspicuous as to be noticeable from half a block away. Mort watched Gordon trot across the boulevard, hop over the painted centre line, and disappear into the Jewish General's emergency entrance.

A jaywalking pedestrian was a scene Mort had witnessed a million times on the streets of Montreal. But watching Gordon through the windshield of his car lope effortlessly across busy Côte-Sainte-Catherine, fairly took Mort's breath away. He experienced a peculiar interval, almost transcendent in its lasting impression. Gordon's movements had been unexpectedly graceful and lively. It made Mort feel, by contrast, like dead weight insulated in the protective bubble of his cumbersome vehicle.

When the traffic light turned green, Mort advanced slowly, all the while asking himself if it was really Gordon that he'd seen? He wasn't so sure anymore. The way the figure had moved and vanished was almost ghostlike. If it was indeed Gordon, why was he going to the hospital? Was it to visit someone? Or was it possible that Gordon was himself sick and was going to see his physician? Gordon did not look like a sick man. Not the way he'd leaped across the busy boulevard. On the contrary, Gordon was the picture of health, although, Mort knew how pictures sometimes didn't tell the whole story. On countless occasions he'd heard about acquaintances, from business or from the old neighbourhood, who were as fit as Jack LaLanne one week and stiffs on the eighth tee at Elm Ridge the next. Gordon was well-known in the community as a book reviewer. He was probably being a *mensch*, going to the hospital to pay a visit on an ailing acquaintance. But Mort had to admit that it was more than that. Gordon hadn't merely walked across the street to visit the sick — an unpleasant task no matter how you sliced it — but *leaped* across the street to do so. As much as he viscerally disliked Gordon, Mort had to admire the extra effort. It added to his sinking feeling that from his vantage point ensconced inside his luxury vehicle it was not he who was passing the world outside, but rather the world was passing him by.

"Oh."

The hollow syllable involuntarily escaped Rusty's mouth and hung in the air between father and daughter for what seemed like minutes.

"Pa."

Mort stood silently on the duplex doorstep feeling as unwelcome as a census-taker.

"Is everything okay?" Rusty said wiping her hands with a red-and-white checkered dish towel. "I mean, you never visit during the day." Rusty was thinking *you've never visited my home, period. Not even once.* Theirs was an almost exclusively telephone relationship.

"I was thinking that it was about time. I hope you don't mind."

"No. No, no, of course not. Please come in. My home is your home. Just try to ignore the mess."

Mort was still not sure why he'd come to Rusty's. When the steering wheel of the Jag turned off Côte-Sainte-Catherine onto Decelles Avenue and inexplicably made a right onto Van Horne it seemed to be operating with a mind of its own. By the time Mort had hit the Wilderton Shopping Center it became clear where he was heading: left on Wilderton, down the hill, and right onto Rusty's street, Bedford Road. He'd found a parking spot right in front of her door. Mort hadn't been sure which doorbell to press, top or bottom. After a short deliberation he'd guessed the top and had waited anxiously with his hand on the door handle for a buzz that would gain him entry. Instead, he heard footsteps coming down a flight of stairs and leaned against the door slightly. It opened by itself.

"What's the matter with your buzzer?" Mort said to Rusty's back as he followed her inside and up the stairs. Rusty wore a long woollen skirt and a plain beige blouse. Her head was covered by a *schmatta* knotted at the base of her skull. As Mort spoke to the back of the *schmatta* he thought about how Rusty had looked on the night of her sweet sixteen party at Ruby Foo's; her smile, spoiled by thick metallic braces — the orthodontist had lied when he promised they'd be off in time for the party — framed in strawberry-blond Farrah Fawcett flips. She wore a Le Chateau tube top decorated in gold sequins that showed off her pale, freckled shoulders, paired with tight, silver satin disco pants. He regretted the thought that this would be the most glamorous mental image of Rusty that Mort was destined to possess for the rest of his life.

"Oh, that. That buzzer's been broken ever since we moved in."

"Why don't you have the landlord fix it?"

"We've asked. It's no big deal."

"No big deal? It's your safety. Doesn't your husband care about his family's safety?"

The subtle dig had slipped out. Standing outside her house, Mort had promised himself that he wouldn't as much as think a nasty thought about Mendel Fuchs, a husband who preferred learning Torah to properly supporting his family.

"It's a safe neighbourhood. Most people around here leave their doors unlocked."

Rusty had inherited none of her mother's fastidiousness. Toys were strewn across the foyer's hardwood floor. A heavy chemical mustiness permeated the apartment, an odour that combined dusty old books and laundry detergent. A vacuum cleaner stood idle in the centre of the living-room area rug and next to it was a toddler's playpen. Mort saw the head of a little girl peeking out over the top of the playpen as if she were a small animal nosing her way cautiously out of a dark burrow. The girl stared at Mort. He smiled back uneasily. Suddenly, flying down the hallway, Mort heard the high-pitched whistle of an oncoming dive-bomber; a boy holding a fighter jet at eye level came hurtling straight for him. The jet dodged past imaginary enemies and manoeuvered into position to fire on target, which appeared to be Mort's crotch. It was a near miss, to Mort's relief. The jet winged past him into the open air of the living room. Mort watched the pilot, his skullcap askew and *tzitzit* bouncing from his waist, expertly navigate around the vacuum cleaner and circle the playpen. The little girl instinctively ducked for cover as the plane zoomed past.

"Look, Ezra, Leorah! Look who came for a visit. It's Zaydie."

For a moment Mort wasn't sure who his daughter was referring to. They'd never firmly settled on Mort being called *Zaydie* and it made him feel uncomfortable. If anything, he thought of himself more as a *Grandpa* or *Papa. Zaydie* sounded old and foreign. The bewildered look on the fighter pilot's face echoed Mort's thinking.

Who is Zaydie? it seemed to say. The little girl gradually peeked out of the playpen to size up the intruder, too.

"The other children are in school," Rusty said. "Why don't you go into the living room and have a seat. I'll bring some tea. It'll just take a few minutes." She disappeared into the kitchen. Mort wasn't interested in having tea. He knew Rusty was improvising, trying to be hospitable. He decided he would play along, anyway.

As Mort entered the living room, the Jewish fighter pilot made a loop-the-loop and landed himself and his aircraft behind the low, rectangular couch in front of the window. He did not come out. *Refuelling*, Mort thought. At the same time, the little girl slid back down inside her playpen. In the minutes that followed, Mort was carefully observed from behind camouflage by two sets of tiny, suspicious eyes.

The armchair Mort sat in squeaked and creaked under his shifting weight. The outdated rectangular couch that provided the fighter pilot shelter was covered in faded green velvet and a half-dozen hideously-coloured decorative pillows, ranging from puke yellow to antifreeze blue. Portraits adorned the walls of the living room in chintzy gold-painted frames; a *minyan* of men with sunken cheeks and moist, sagging eyes, all wearing large black hats and sporting long, white beards. Famous rabbis, Mort surmised from their dark uniforms and world-weary half smiles. Bookshelves covered one wall from floor to ceiling filled with dozens and dozens of tall, leather-bound religious tomes, their spines embossed in gold Hebrew lettering: several versions of the Five Books of Moses, volumes of the Talmud, Tehillim, the Zohar, various books of rabbinic commentaries, by Rashi, the Rambam, the Chofetz Chaim, and a volume of the Tanya. On another smaller shelf, less prominently located, were inspirational religious writings in English with titles like *Bringing Heaven Down To Earth*, *Principles of the Good Life*, *A Treasury of Chassidic Tales*, *The Infinite Light*, and *Fingerprints on the Universe*.

Everything about these surroundings made Mort feel like a foreigner, from the musty, outdated, Salvation Army decor, to the shelves of books, to the tiny, leery eyes that observed him from behind the protective cover of furniture. His body sunk uncomfortably into the armchair. Unbidden, a well-known Biblical phrase, as if it had travelled on an invisible air current from the bookshelves on the other side of the room, mysteriously entered Mort's head. *And God said to Abram "Get thee out of thy country, and from thy kin, and from thy father's house, unto the land that I will show thee."*

Mort had been dumbfounded by Rusty's decision to reject the lifestyle and comforts she'd enjoyed growing up in Hampstead. He'd taken it personally. It was not just a repudiation of her upbringing, where she'd come from, and who she was, but of her father, too, everything he'd worked so hard to build and provide for his family. It hurt him. He looked around the room at the life she had made for herself, the one she had chosen, and slumping in his chair shook his head.

And yet a force had steered him here. It could not be religion. Mort was not a religious person and he certainly wasn't going to start now. It didn't matter that the deference with which Rusty treated him was calculated based on her religious need to abide the Fifth Commandment. He appreciated the calls every Friday and the concern she showed. Despite their differences, Mort knew that he and Rusty were on the same page in regards to Jackie's lifestyle and decision to get married. Father and daughter, as it turned out, had common ground. The bottom line would always be that they were family. If nothing else, that fact alone could be counted on to provide an ample starting point for whatever came next in their relationship.

Now, if only Mort could figure out how to get beyond the feeling that he was a stranger in a strange land, or rather, a strange living room. He wondered if he could coax the children out of hiding the way tourists did in the Third World countries they visited. Mort shifted his hips forward and dug his hand into his pocket bringing out a fistful of coins.

"Hey, Sonny boy! Captain! You want to see something?" Mort held up a shiny dollar coin between his thumb and forefinger in the direction of the ugly couch. "Why don't you come out and I'll give you a brand-new coin."

No takers.

"A little *Chanukah gelt*. I know it's early for that, but you can put it away for safekeeping until holiday time."

Nothing.

"So, it'll be birthday money."

Still nothing.

"Here. I'll tell you what. I have a prettier coin for you. A two-dollar coin. You can have both coins if you like. That's three dollars. Nothing to sneeze at. Three dollars will get you a lot of candy at the store," Mort said, though he wasn't sure how much candy you could get for three dollars these days. He waved the two coins in the air. Still no movement from behind the couch.

Mort noticed his granddaughter peeking over the edge of the playpen. The bait was being taken. He pushed himself up from the armchair and slowly made his away to the centre of the room.

"Finally, someone with sense," Mort said, feeling relieved. "So you'd like some *gelt*, honey. "Now, Zaydie," — Mort hesitated on the word — "Zaydie sees who got the practical genes, from Zaydie's side of the family." The girl's thin arm reached out of the playpen and her frail fingers unfolded like petals of a delicate flower. Mort's golden coin filled the centre of her palm. It remained there for only a second, until Rusty entered the room.

"What in heaven's name are you doing?" Hot water splashed as Rusty put the teapot down in a hurry. "You can't give her money. She'll put it in her mouth!" Which, no sooner had the words been uttered, is exactly where the coin went.

At that moment a supersonic aircraft screeched to life from behind the couch. It took off as if from the platform of a seafaring aircraft carrier and tore a path across the room, sliding in between Mort and the playpen. Startled, Mort lost his footing and fell against the playpen, knocking his granddaughter flat on her back. Simultaneously, Rusty, who was advancing to get the coin out of Leorah's mouth, tripped and landed on top of her father next to the playpen. Leorah's eyes stared up at the ceiling, her chest heaved, but no sound came out.

The jet circled the wreckage, searching for survivors.

eleven

"Zaydie ... Zaydie ... you dead?"

"Leave Zaydie alone, Ezra. Let him rest."

"*Now* can I have the money?" Ezra said, shoving his face close to Mort's.

It had taken some time to find the coin under the bookshelves. In the commotion of toppling bodies, no one noticed the tiny golden disc being spat out across the room as Leorah was jostled to the bottom of her playpen. There were tense moments; Leorah trying to catch her breath and finally letting out a wail, Rusty digging frantically inside the playpen to find the physical proof that the coin hadn't been ingested, and Mort moaning on the floor. The playpen was flipped upside down and shaken. When nothing fell out, Rusty began crawling on all fours around the room like a sniffing hound, a sight that sent both Ezra and Leorah into simultaneous giggling fits.

"I'm calling an ambulance," Rusty said once the coin had been retrieved and she was attending to her father who remained immobile on the floor next to the playpen.

"No, please don't. It's not necessary. Just let me rest here a few minutes."

"Can I at least get you something?"

"No. I'm fine."

"Let me help you to the couch."

"It's probably just a bruise," Mort said between groans as Rusty clutched his arm and pulled him delicately up off the floor.

"I'll get you an extra-strength Aspirin."

Rusty collected three pillows and tucked them under her father's head as he lay on the couch. Feeling drowsy and assailed by the stench of unwashed upholstery, Mort dozed off in a few minutes.

He was wakened after an hour by Ezra asking if he was dead.

"You really got me, eh? I like your style, Captain," Mort said groggily. "Very clever, letting the little girl be your decoy and then swooping in for the score. 'Course I have a coin for you, too. Just don't let your sister get her greedy little hands on it." Mort winced with the effort of getting his hand in and out of his pocket.

"I'm heading home," he said to Rusty, who watched doubtfully as Mort lifted his head off the pillows and struggled to swing his feet to the floor. "I'll be okay. It's just a bruise." But Mort wasn't so sure. He might have cracked a rib or two. As sore as he felt, his side throbbing with every movement, Mort wanted to leave Rusty's as soon as possible, before Mendel and the rest of her clan got home and the place became a real zoo. His tolerance for mayhem had reached its limit.

"If it wasn't for Ezra and Leorah, I would insist on driving you to the hospital to get checked."

"I'll be fine. You've got your hands full right here."

Careful not to make any sudden movements, Mort made it up the elevator without too much suffering. A double Crown Royal on the rocks would relax his muscles and numb the lingering pain. The quiet of his apartment had never sounded so good. He slipped daintily out of his clothes. In boxers and undershirt — he wasn't about to attempt a Houdini-like contortion to escape his undershirt — he set himself down in slow-motion into the recliner, mentally prepared to stay there for a long while. He wondered if he would ever be capable of getting up again. Grimacing, he reached over for the Crown Royal bottle and lifted it in the air to visually estimate how long his supply would last. If the situation grew desperate he'd have to call down to the doorman to fetch another bottle. It wouldn't be the first time.

Deciding that it was unwise to be disturbed while he convalesced, Mort ignored the flashing red message indicator on the telephone for the next few days. It only took one day before he felt well enough to shower, slip into an Adidas tracksuit, and slip out to the liquor store around the corner. He also picked up a few essentials at the grocery store, some chocolate-covered marshmallow cookies, one box of crackers, a wedge of cheddar (on sale), three cans of salmon, and a loaf of white bread. Back upstairs and feeling resupplied, Mort was desert-island ready to stay home incommunicado for a long while. The buzz of the telephone caught him off guard. The front desk was calling. A police officer was asking permission to come upstairs.

"Well, at least he's polite," Mort said, hanging up the phone. In the two minutes it took for Mort to hide the Crown Royal bottle and dump his empty glasses in the kitchen sink, Potente appeared at his apartment door.

"I phoned and left messages," he said, an expression of concern painted on his face. "Several times."

"I had a bit of an accident. I've been recuperating." Mort knew that the air inside the apartment was stale and reeked of alcohol. He hesitated to invite the arson investigator inside.

"Are you all right?"

"Yes." Mort's mouth was dry and his breath sour. Scratching at his unshaven chin, Mort couldn't remember the last time he'd brushed his teeth.

"I wanted to speak to you. About the case. Do you mind if I come in?"

Now it was a *case*. "Not at all," Mort lied. "Please excuse the way things look."

"I don't mean to bother you in your home, Mr. Halbman. I won't stay long." Potente strolled casually past Mort and into the living room, apparently unbothered by the odour. "It's about the ownership of 92 Hampstead Road," he added, dropping himself onto the leather sofa. He extended his arm along the furniture's back, making himself at home. Mort plopped himself down in his recliner, but didn't lean backward to kick up the leg rest.

"We knew from the deed of sale that the purchaser was a numbered company. As you probably know, it's not unusual for a company to hold the deed on a family home. In the case of Hampstead Road, the purchasing company was not a Quebec or Canadian corporation. It was Bahamian. An offshore corporation. That can send up a red flag."

"Red flag? What sort of red flag?"

"I'm sure you know why offshore corporations are sometimes created. Something less than kosher going on behind the scenes."

Why did the Italian use the word "kosher"? Mort wondered. It was an uncharacteristic choice of words, filled with innuendo. "What does an offshore corporation have to do with the fire? Are you working for the taxman or something?" Mort said breathlessly, immediately regretting that he might have sounded shrill and defensive.

"What I meant to say, Officer Potente," Mort continued in more measured tones, "was that I thought you guys in arson were concerned with fires, not tax evasion."

"I didn't say anything about tax evasion," Potente answered.

"You implied it. We all know that offshore corporations are often used for that purpose."

"No. You're right. That sort of thing doesn't interest us in arson. That's the purview of federal and provincial authorities. Only, sometimes a suspicious transaction *can* indicate motivation for a crime, an attempt to defraud the insurance company, for example."

"Jewish lightning," Mort said.

"Yes, that kind of activity." Potente smiled, remembering when he'd mentioned Jewish lightning to Mort earlier.

"Are you saying that the investigation found evidence of arson?"

"No. Not yet. We're still unsure about the cause."

"I suppose you know that it's gone," Mort said.

"Gone?"

"Yes. The house. It's been torn down and carted away."

"Oh, yes. The demolition required our approval once our collection of physical evidence from the scene was completed. Laboratory examination is underway as we speak. It shouldn't be long before we have some final answers on the cause. Which brings me to you."

"Me?"

"Well, not exactly you. Your son. I believe congratulations are in order. You must be very proud."

Mort felt a family of skittering rodents excavate the pit of his alcohol-shrunk stomach.

"Officer Potente," he interjected, not wanting to hear what the cop was about to say next. "May I call you Massimo?"

"Sure."

"Massimo. I was thinking about the first time we met outside 92. We talked about where you grew up, in Saint Leonard."

"Yes, I remember."

"Well ... if it's not too much trouble ... and you have a bit of spare time ... I was wondering if you could take me there."

"Take you? Where?"

"To Saint Leo. Your neighbourhood. Where you grew up. I haven't been there in ages. The last time was probably to buy some pastries. Great pastry shops out there, if I recall. We can talk about other topics along the way."

"All right," Potente said.

"I meant, right *now.*"

It had been a quiet ride. Driver and passenger didn't continue their conversation from Mort's apartment. Mort stared out at the afternoon gridlock on the Metropolitan Autoroute in a daze, ignoring the flashing, beeping raft of dashboard police gadgetry, a tiny computer screen attached to a buzzing radio headset. Potente broke the silence once with a *"Vah-fungoo!"* to another driver who cut in front of the van without signalling. Mort jumped in his seat. Then he grinned, feeling more at ease.

The exit for Saint Leonard was approaching. The endless number of car dealerships lining the autoroute told Mort so. One after another, huge billboards advertised every brand of vehicle: Japanese, Korean, German, Italian, and American, running the gamut of quality and price. Pontiac, Buick, GMC, Chrysler, Volvo, Toyota, Nissan, Subaru, Acura, Honda, Suzuki, Volkswagen, Hyundai, Porsche, and Lamborghini. Then, rising out of the chaos of clamouring automotive commerce there was a jungle-green sign for British-made Land Rover and perched on a column above it, was a twenty-foot-long, polished silver jaguar, a mammoth replica of Mort's stolen hood ornament. It looked like the figure atop a monumental championship sports trophy. A feeling of fatigue gave way to a sense of relief. Mort felt as if he'd been running a marathon and finally crossed the victory line. He said aloud, "Can we …?" then stopped himself, watching the Jaguar dealership zoom past. "Never mind," he muttered under his breath, sinking back into his seat.

Potente hadn't heard.

The maroon police van exited the Metropolitan at Viau Street. The streetlight at Jean-Talon came into view within less than a minute.

Jean-Talon was a street that told a whole story when you travelled it from one end to the other. Actually, make that many stories. It was among the longest streets on the island of Montreal, almost as long as St. Catherine, but without the downtown thoroughfare's cosmopolitan cache. It wasn't a destination, or where events happened that you read about in the newspaper. Jean-Talon was where people *lived*. Working-class families shopped and raised children in the districts traversed by the street. Jean-Talon touched the Decarie Expressway in the west and ended at the Galeries D'Anjou shopping centre in the east. In between, it connected five Metro stations from different north-south lines and strung together several boroughs. The Greeks of Park Extension might justifiably claim Jean-Talon as their own. Hellenic restaurants, souvenir stores, and clothing shops dotted the street east of L'Acadie Boulevard. But no community could lay claim to it like the Italians, the single-most heavily populated ethnic group in Montreal. At its halfway point, Jean-Talon delimited Little Italy, with its trendy cafés and grocery stores. Farther on, it ran directly through the heart of Saint Leonard, *Città Italiana*, where Mort and Officer Potente were headed. Some locals called the Saint Leonard section of Jean-Talon *Via Italia*.

The van slowed to a stop near the corner of Jean-Talon across from a McDonald's, in front of a recently constructed, nondescript, beige residential building. "This," Potente said to Mort, shifting the vehicle into Park, "is our first stop."

On the entrance canopy of the building, written in cursive, it said *Domaine Atrium*.

"A condominium building?" Mort said, puzzled.

"A seniors' residence. But do not be deceived," Potente exclaimed. "The Casa Mina once stood here. One of the wildest strip clubs in town. They had girls dancing for the men on the ground floor, and men dancing for the ladies on the second floor."

"What happened to it?"

"They tore it down after the owner's son got whacked."

"Whacked?"

"Killed. About five years ago. I went to high school with the guy. He was a mean sonofabitch. Drove a Maserati convertible to class in our senior year."

Potente shifted the van into gear and made a left-hand turn onto Jean-Talon. Two-storey buildings lined the street with stores on the bottom and apartments on top. There were hair salons, dry cleaners, triple-X video rental stores, pastry shops, and at every second corner, a café.

"Ha, take a look here," Potente said excitedly. The van turned into the alleyway next to a pastry shop. In the window were a half-dozen pink-and-white four-tier wedding cakes decorated in baby-blue and yellow cream flowers and topped with heart-framed miniature plastic brides and grooms.

"They beat the original owner of this place with sandbags."

"Sandbags?"

"Yeah, breaks bones without leaving marks. They forced him to sell. The guy who owns it now calls the shots. Never heard of the Montreal pastry wars?"

"I'm guessing it wasn't over who had the best recipe."

"Reception halls. This guy was the big winner. Ended up controlling the entire racket." Potente pointed to another pastry shop directly across the street that displayed an equally impressive array of wedding cakes. "That one burned down twice. But I guess they settled their differences. He learned not to step on too many toes. Rough business, making cannoli." The van backed out of the driveway onto Jean-Talon.

"Now I'll take you to see the local fire station."

Turning on Lacordaire Boulevard, they passed a large park where Mort saw a mob of boys wearing numbered blue-and-red striped shirts and knee-high socks running around in multiple directions. Next to the soccer pitch, groups of grey-haired men lobbed fist-sized bocce balls from one end of a long rectangular sandbox to the other. On the sidelines, their cohort watched in deep concentration, arms akimbo, preparing to render judgment on shots made and missed. Mort noticed a monument at the centre of the park, a large silver figure atop an oblong concrete pedestal. It appeared to be a marching soldier. As the van got closer. Mort saw that the man wasn't dressed in military fatigues. He wore a jacket and slacks, and, in place of a bayonet, he swung a briefcase at his side.

"What's that?"

"A tribute to our hero. The Italian immigrant businessman who built this community."

Mort remembered whose side of the war the Italians had fought on. They weren't likely to have a Second World War monument in Saint Leonard.

A left turn brought the van into a small driveway on a prime piece of real estate at a busy intersection near the highway. They pulled up to the base of a massive billboard announcing a future condo development with pictures of luxury living rooms and shiny kitchens at unreasonably low "Starting At" prices.

"There used to be a coffee-and-donuts franchise right where we're sitting," said Potente. "It went bust, and a few years later a Greek guy bought the building and renovated it for a restaurant. It wasn't a secret. The construction took months. He put up a huge sign with pictures, like the one you see here. Spent a fortune on the building too; art-deco design, plush furniture, stainless steel, and wrought-iron ornaments. Less than a week after the restaurant opened, it burned to the ground. And not just *to the ground*. It was completely incinerated. There was nothing left in the morning but ash and dust. The firemen didn't make it on time."

"I thought you were taking me to see the local fire station," Mort said.

Potente put the van in reverse and twisted the steering wheel to turn the vehicle around. Directly down the street, barely a stone's throw away, two sets of polished chrome square headlights stared out from the fire station's wide-open garage doors. "The firemen could have left their trucks parked in the station and dragged the hoses here. That's how close it is." Potente chuckled. "Poor guy didn't get the *right* permission."

This guided tour was not the warm and fuzzy homecoming Mort had expected it would be. He was beginning to get nervous.

"Maybe we can see …"

"Wait. Just one more," Potente said. "This one you've *got* to see."

In three minutes, they were back on Jean-Talon, rolling up to a pizza franchise.

Potente pointed through the windshield, "You see that pizza joint we're approaching? I remember when they built it, the first time."

"The first time?"

"Yeah, that's the third version. They burned down the other two. But that's not why I brought you here. The second time they torched it, the explosion blew the oven clear across the parking lot and through the front door of that drugstore, way over there. Do you have any idea how much a pizza oven weighs? Landed like a bomb."

"Massimo, I was thinking we might see other sites — less *infamous* ones. Like how about the street where you grew up?"

"Sure. It's not far. I just thought that you might be interested in … you know … fires, considering what happened to your house." Potente sounded hesitant, like he had something on his mind that he was holding back intentionally.

The van turned around and cruised east on Jean-Talon past café after café.

"So many cafés," Mort remarked.

"We call them 'bars.' Italian men spend more time in the bars than they do at home. They all have *their* bar — one that they're fiercely loyal to."

"Do you have a bar? One that's *yours?*"

"We all had one growing up. The bar was where we met our friends, watched soccer matches, talked about business and politics."

"There are so many of them. How do they all survive?"

"Not by selling espresso."

"What else do they sell?"

"Anything."

"Anything?"

"If there's one thing to be said for Italians, it's that we love to live well," Potente said proudly. "We love to have the fastest cars, the most delicious food, the finest clothes, the most beautiful women, the biggest weddings, you name it."

"And you can get any of those things at the bar?"

"If you couldn't find it elsewhere, or it was too expensive, at the bar there was always a guy who knew a guy who knew someone — you get the picture."

"Uh-huh."

The van turned down a residential street. "I'm not going to point out my mom's house," Potente said. "Security concerns, you understand. This street is exactly like the one where I grew up."

They passed block after block of attached 1960s-era white brick duplexes, all with brand-new or freshly painted balcony railings and compact lush gardens blooming curbside. The homes were well-maintained and identical, except for small defining features — the ornate design of the front door, a garden statue, or the colour and variety of flowers.

"My mom used to work for Jews," Potente said. "She did piecework for a childrenswear company. Sewing machines were hooked up in our garage and operated by a group of ladies from the neighbourhood. A guy named Saulie would drop off bags of clothes and pick them up once they were finished. After school, I remember squeezing snaps onto bundles of clothes while watching TV. Sometimes Saulie hung around until my mom would feed him. He loved her homemade cannelloni. Occasionally, he showed up without a bag of clothes, around dinnertime."

"Is it close?" Mort asked.

"Is what close?"

"Your bar. Where a guy knows a guy who knows someone ..."

"I don't follow you."

"You said that you can get anything at the bar."

"Yeah."

"Does that include car parts?"

"You want to know if you can you get car parts at the bar?"

"Yeah."

"Probably."

"What about stolen car parts?"

"Yeah, probably."

"I have this problem," Mort explained. "The hood ornament on my Jaguar was stolen in my garage. I've been thinking about how to replace it. On the way here, when we drove past the Jaguar dealership, it rang bells. I thought about asking you to stop the van. Only, a brand-new hood ornament from the dealer would cost a fortune. Then you said you could get anything at your bar."

"Okay, let me get this straight. You're asking *me* to help you get a hood ornament for your Jaguar on the black market?"

"I wouldn't want you to get into trouble, Massimo. I certainly couldn't just walk into a bar myself, a complete stranger, and ask for a Jaguar hood ornament. You, on the other hand, you're from the neighbourhood, and a cop to boot. I was thinking that you could at least make inquiries on my behalf."

Mort wondered if the Italians had a word for *chutzpah*.

twelve

Aside from the three ignored messages left by Officer Potente on Mort's answering service, there were four others. Three were from Gerstein. When he got back from Saint Leonard Mort listened to them with mild interest. The last message on the machine, however, elicited an immediate response.

"Mort, we really missed you at the El Morocco. I'm sorry that you couldn't make it and hope everything is all right." Mona sounded genuinely concerned. Her pre-emptive phone call made Mort feel like a total shit, a coward for not showing up at the restaurant, and an idiot for not calling her earlier to apologize. "I'd appreciate if you could give me a call."

Mort didn't hesitate. Feeling anxious, his heart pounding, he dialled her number before sitting down.

"Hello."

"Mort?"

"Yeah. Hi."

"Hi. How are you?"

"Look, I'm sorry, about the restaurant. I wasn't feeling well.

It came over me at the very last second, there ..."

"It's okay. Don't worry about it ..."

"There wasn't enough time to cancel ..."

"Don't worry. I'm sorry that you missed it. We had a good time. Are you feeling better?"

"Yes. A bit." Mort's side still throbbed from the spill he'd taken at Rusty's.

"Noah's parents are very nice, dignified people. I think you would have gotten along well with Albert, the father. He's in the outerwear business. He and Gordon had a great deal to talk about, too. He's an educated man. They discussed Proust and Camus. It was quite thrilling to hear them."

"I hope there was no offense taken," Mort said.

"They were concerned for your well-being."

"And Jackie?"

"He was disappointed. But once the food was served and the occasion was toasted your absence wasn't mentioned again."

"I'm going to call him."

"I think he would appreciate that." There was a pause. "Mort, can I be honest with you?"

"Okay."

"We never communicated well when we were married. Sometimes I think that getting a divorce was our last stab at trying to make ourselves heard to one another," Mona chuckled. Mort didn't chuckle back. "I want you to hear what I'm about to say without feeling attacked. Okay? I mean, at this stage of the game we're beyond defensiveness, don't you agree?"

"Okay."

"It's not the first time that you've disappointed Jacob. I wonder if, just this once, you could put your disappointments aside to be there for your son."

"What's that supposed to mean?"

"You've been disappointed your whole life, Mort. I'm not sure why. I mean what do you have to be disappointed about?

You've got two healthy, successful kids. You're relatively healthy yourself. You live in financial comfort. There are so many people worse off than you."

"So?"

"So, now your son wants to share an important event in his life, a milestone — a milestone in all our lives, really. It's important that you're supportive. I know you're disappointed by the way Jacob leads his life. All I'm asking Mort is, for once, let this not be about *your* disappointment. Try to acknowledge Jacob's chosen path."

"Jacob's chosen path?" Mona was reverting to psychobabble again.

"How can I put this in another way?" Mona said. "What if God had a plan?"

"God?" Mort had never heard Mona mention *Him* before.

"I know that you don't like talking about religion. It hasn't been a particular interest of mine either until recently. Anyway, humour me for a minute."

She's got God on the brain because she's been interviewing rabbis for the wedding.

"Supposing God existed and He had a plan?" Mona asked.

"God's plan?"

"Right. That would mean that every person had a special role to play."

"In God's plan?"

"Yes."

Hold on. "God's plan" didn't sound like it came from a gay wedding rabbi. It was something a holier-than-thou, black-hat rabbi would say. Mona's been reading Rusty's books.

"No one knows their individual role —"

"In God's plan?

"Yes," Mona replied. "How it makes sense in the grand scheme of things. That's the nature of God. We can't know His plan because that would mean we possess God's knowledge."

God's plan. God's knowledge. Mort couldn't believe what he was hearing. He was positive that Mona had been dipping into Rusty's library. "Mona, what are you talking about? Have you lost your mind?"

"Please, Mort. Just humour me."

"Not knowing our role in God's plan — really, Mona. It's a load of nonsense."

"Not to everyone."

Mort immediately understood the reference to their daughter.

"Trust me on this, Mort. Go with me."

"Okay, so God has a plan and we can't know our role in it."

"Right."

"So where the hell does that leave us?" Mort said.

"Well ..."

"I'll tell where!" Mort interrupted. "Nowhere! That's where!"

"Or somewhere," Mona responded softly.

"What does that mean? *Somewhere?*"

"You're nowhere if you don't *trust*."

"Trust?"

"Yes."

"Trust who? Trust God?"

"Well, no. Not necessarily. Trust is the foundation of all meaningful living. If you don't believe in God you can start by trusting the people closest to you. Mort — and again, please take this in the spirit in which it's meant — you have difficulty trusting. Always have. You never trusted me when we were married. And you don't trust your kids. Whether you like it or not, they have made up their own minds about how they will live their lives. You always treated your family like it was a business, an investment on which you expected a certain return. Creating a family, building a *home*, doesn't pay off, at least, not the way a business does. If you *trust* the people closest to you, the people who truly love you, it will pay dividends in its own way."

The people who truly love you. The words unexpectedly resonated with Mort. He didn't hear the rest of what Mona said, nor did he react when she finished. For once, he had nothing to say to Mona. No instant retort or remark. He didn't feel attacked, or hurt, or defensive. In a cosmic instance he went from feeling ready to burst, to feeling nothing at all, a black hole inside. Then, in the time it took for silence to fill his telephone connection with Mona, Mort welled up with emotion. He could swear Mona had told him that *she* loved him. He was overcome. Tears blurred his vision.

"Do you understand what I'm trying to say, Mort?"

"I think so," he said, choking-up.

"I really hope you can join us next time."

"Next time?" Mort swallowed hard and coughed.

"Yes. Hopefully, you'll feel better. There'll be other occasions to meet the family before the wedding."

Mort didn't think he could contain the urge to sob for much longer. Two more words and the floodgates would open. He said, "Bye" and slapped the receiver down on its base.

After showering and shaving, Mort returned Gerstein's calls. All three messages that he'd left on the answering service were about Sandy. *Better get this over with,* he thought.

Gerstein did most of the talking, as usual. He told Mort that he'd been panicked since their last phone call. He'd been getting ready to call the cops when he didn't hear back from Mort after a few days. "More cops are all I need," Mort muttered.

Gerstein described how low Mort had sounded at Snowdon Deli, using the word *suicidal.* "Not since Blue Monday ..." he said. Mort smirked. Of course, Gerstein possessed the antidote to Mort's blues: the companionship of a certain lady. Mort was getting ready to block the discussion, throw up a detour sign, say something to shift the flow in another direction, but Gerstein wouldn't let him. He blabbered on, making the case for his sister. Within a few minutes, in spite of himself, Mort found that he was agreeing with his buddy. Yes, Sandy was a wonderful person. Yes, she was fit and looked good for her age. Yes, she was intelligent, kind, hardworking, and independent. Yes, yes, yes. All the yes-ing cheered up Mort. Then Gerstein slipped in, "So will you take her out?" and Mort answered "Yes" without thinking. He could have retracted. But Mort figured that it was the only surefire way of shutting up Gerstein once and for all. There was another reason for sticking to his "yes." It was related to what Mona had said about *trusting the people closest to you.* Gerstein was one of those *closest* people to Mort, had been for all these years. His pestering and pleading showed that he genuinely cared. Taking Sandy on a date, a relatively painless gesture, would show his old buddy how much he appreciated their friendship.

Gerstein could hardly contain his enthusiasm. He insisted on acting as their go-between. Mort was suddenly awash in doubt. What did one do on a date nowadays? Where did one take a woman of Sandy's age? Surely, going on a date meant that they had to actually *go* somewhere? The phrase "on a date" made Mort shudder. She didn't seem like the restaurant type — not a *decent* restaurant, anyway, like the Bar-B-Barn or Le Bifthèque. Should he take her to a movie? Mort hadn't been to a cinema in twenty-five years. He had no interest in the current Hollywood offering of space aliens, school-age wizards, comic-book superheroes, and tits-obsessed frat boys making fart jokes. He reckoned that Sandy felt the same way. She'd probably prefer going for a stroll up on Mount-Royal. Mort didn't think he was physically up to that challenge. His weak ankle might give out. Under different circumstances he would have relied on advice from his best friend. Having Gerstein as his matchmaker disqualified him.

The solution hit Mort like a blast of cool air on a sweltering summer day. "Ask your sister if she has a valid passport," Mort said.

Gerstein wanted to know why. "Planning a romantic getaway to Cuba?"

"Never mind," said Mort, "just ask her and call me back. Also, find out if she's available this coming Saturday afternoon."

Gerstein's job as Mort and Sandy's intermediary wasn't easy. Sandy didn't appreciate being kept in the dark about why she needed a valid passport for her outing with Mort. She called her brother repeatedly to tell him that she was seriously considering backing out of the date unless he came up with an explanation. Gerstein questioned Mort, who remained evasive. Finally, Mort told Gerstein to tell Sandy that they'd be taking a drive through the countryside. She responded suspiciously that it was a little early to see the foliage changing colours, but didn't push the matter further after her brother said that her lack of trust was beginning to offend him personally.

It was the countryside, indeed, that Mort had in mind; the clear lakes and green mountains of Vermont. He was a silent partner in a failing restaurant in St. Albans, a town located an hour and a half south of Montreal. The Smiling Steer was a steak and ribs joint between Pie in the Sky Pizzeria and Yankee One Dollar in the strip mall just off Interstate 89. It had a sizable dining room and a bar at the back that featured live country music Thursday through Saturday, nights that were popular with the truckers. The dining room was a break-even proposition, but the bar was profitable.

Mort needed to own a restaurant like he needed a hole in the head. That was his first reaction when Irna Ginch approached him with the idea. Owning a restaurant required long hours and eagle-eye surveillance. Then again, Mort knew that he couldn't refuse a request from the buyer of The Dress Shack, Halbman Dress's third best customer.

For years, Irna's husband Stan had dreamed of owning a Vermont eatery. He was a romantic who talked of having a kitchen that featured regional dishes, and fresh, grain-fed meats from local farms. When a fully equipped establishment became available in St. Albans, he jumped at the opportunity. Stan needed a financial backer and his wife was determined to find him one. Mort persuaded his brother that Irna would make their investment worthwhile. Even if The Smiling Steer turned out to be a dud, he argued, a healthy return on their $100,000 would come from increased dress sales, which is exactly what happened. From one year to the next, Irna rewarded Mort by cutting Halbman Dress a larger portion of her dress department's purchasing budget. The Dress Shack quickly rose to become Halbman Dress's number-one customer. As a bonus, Stan Ginch proved himself a capable bar/restaurant owner. Both dress *and* beer profits filled Halbman's coffers.

For the last year, however, income from the restaurant had been in steep decline. It was puzzling, particularly during the summer months when beer sales were usually sky-high. Mort suspected that Manfred Goslin, a yokel who tended fifty head of Black Angus by day and the restaurant's bar by night, was stealing him blind. Stan blamed the rise in the Canadian dollar. The country music bands were drawing smaller crowds because the truckers were making fewer export runs from Canada into the States. Also, the margins on their favourite brands of Canadian beer were getting slimmer. The explanations were plausible, but insufficient as far as Mort was concerned. When he accused Goslin of helping himself to the till, Stan emphatically vouched for his employee. Mort remained unconvinced. The overanxious smile Goslin flashed Mort on occasions when he'd drop in to the bar unannounced only added to his suspicion.

The date with Sandy would kill two birds with one stone. He'd take her for an evening drive to St. Albans. They'd park the car on Main Street, get a bite to eat at Manutti's (surely Sandy ate pasta?), and cruise over to the drive-in next to the interstate. When the movie finished (hopefully something he could stomach, a romantic comedy or drama), it would be late. Mort would casually mention that he was part owner of a restaurant nearby. He'd suggest they sneak in to The Smiling Steer for a nightcap, and wham-o, he would nab the thief red-handed.

The plan was foolproof. Well, almost. What would he and Sandy talk about in the car for three hours? She was a fan of exercise, he of rye whisky. Mort decided they would take back roads to cross into the States, scenic Route 202 to the quaint border at Alburg Springs where there was never a lineup. In the soft, salmon hues of early evening light, they'd view Lake Champlain at Missisquoi Bay and enjoy the wetlands and winding river delta that bordered the roadway. The beautiful scenery would provide the main topic of conversation. Failing that, Mort and Sandy did have one other subject in common. If the silences became unbearable they could talk about the escapades of their Stetson-wearing matchmaker.

Gerstein was meticulous. In the days leading up to *the date* he called both parties incessantly to make sure that there was no misunderstanding about pickup time (5:00 p.m.) and attire (casual). He admitted to Mort that he hadn't been this excited since spray-painting obscenities across the front door of Greenbaum's Pharmacy on Queen Mary Road.

"*You* did that?" Mort was shocked. The incident had received front page coverage in both *The Gazette* and *Canadian Jewish News*. Representatives from the national office of B'nai Brith were quoted decrying the rise of anti-Semitism in Canada. "I can't believe you never told me," Mort said.

"I didn't want to implicate you, in case something went wrong," Gerstein told him. "That *putz* screwed over my sister and nephews. I had to do *something*."

* * *

"Are you going to tell me where we're headed," Sandy said, as she slid gracefully into the Jag's passenger seat. "Or are you a psycho killer planning to rape and abandon me in the forests of another country?"

Mort was speechless. Sandy looked radiant, unrecognizably so. The Sandy he'd imagined in the preceding week was a Jewish lady of leisure, a slightly sad woman in designer exercise clothes, anguished by the sight of her triceps-flab. It was a version of Sandy that Mort had deemed acceptable, or rather, he had imagined could accept *him*. By comparison, the Sandy sitting in the leather seat next to him was an imposter. She was elegant, cheery, energetic, and altogether lovely. Gerstein had undersold her.

A hint of perfume greeted Mort as Sandy slammed the car door shut with manly force. She brushed the wrinkles from her form-fitting beige slacks and drew the seatbelt strap across her modest blouse. The wide loops of her crocheted shawl were momentarily tangled in the seatbelt buckle as she tried to click it shut. "Okay, I'm yours," she said smiling broadly and settling into her seat. "So, where're we headed, *mon capitaine?*"

Not a single aspect of Sandy's appearance was overdone. Her skin was taut without looking surgically enhanced. Her makeup was applied naturally — she may have been wearing rouge to bring out her cheekbones, Mort couldn't tell for sure. Auburn highlights accented the wave of her shoulder-length hair.

"Vermont," Mort said.

"I'd guessed either Burlington or Plattsburgh. My money was on New York. It's closer." She squeezed open the gold clasps of the small red leather purse on her lap and extracted her passport to prove that she'd come prepared.

"St. Albans," Mort said, putting the Jag in gear and pulling away from the curb.

Little was said until they were off the island and reached the highway. Mort set the Jag's cruise control at 105, five kilometres an hour over the maximum speed limit. He periodically glanced over at Sandy. "All-terrain flats," she commented, thinking that he was interested in her shoes. "You never said where we were going, so I had to dress for any eventuality." Mort was visually taking measurements. He couldn't ever remember anyone looking so comfortable in his passenger seat. The Jag interior seemed to have been designed with a woman of Sandy's physique and demeanour in mind.

They had plenty to talk about on the drive. Sandy knew the region surrounding their destination quite well. In addition to the countless shopping trips she'd made to Burlington, she'd taken her boys to a farm in Enosburg Falls. The place was owned by a banker originally from Boston who'd chucked it all to become a gentleman farmer. He kept horses and cows and rented rooms to visitors who wanted to have a "farming experience."

As they neared the border at Alburg Springs, Sandy said, "My brother really cares about you, Mort."

"He cares about you, too. I guess that's why we're here. Together."

"I mean, he's been worried about you. Is everything all right?"

"Sure. Why not?"

"Well, he said that you've been distant lately."

Wait a minute. Something was wrong. Mort was doing a favour for his best friend by taking his poor, done-wrong sister out on a date. Why was she asking him if *he* was all right? He wasn't the charity case. Mort felt flushed and sweaty. He turned up the car air conditioning.

"What has your brother been saying about me?" Mort said after a minute.

"Well, like I said, he's been concerned that you haven't been yourself recently."

Gerstein *was* playing double agent.

"So he sent you on a mission!"

"Pardon?"

"He figured that you'd get me to open up! Wasn't that the idea?"

"He said that you'd expressed an interest in spending time with me. That you'd said some nice things about me."

"Asshole." Mort instantly wanted out of this situation.

"Excuse me?"

"Gerstein, that *putz*, told me the same thing about you. He said that you were interested in *me!* Now look where we are!"

The Jag pulled up to a Vermont-style wooden house with a pitched, shingled roof. A holstered firearm appeared inside the frame of Sandy's lowered window followed by a stern face.

"Where're you folks headed?" the border guard demanded.

Mort felt stymied. He knew that hesitating to answer questions at border crossings was a big no-no. "St. Albans," he replied quickly, handing his passport to Sandy, who passed it on together with hers to the officer. "Both Canadian citizens?" the officer said, opening the booklets and vanishing into the house.

"What are we supposed to do now?" Mort said to Sandy in a whisper.

"The purpose of your visit to the United States?" The border guard was back.

"Dinner," Sandy said.

"Are you bringing any alcohol, tobacco, firearms, or anything that you might leave in the country?"

"No," Mort said.

"Enjoy your dinner in St. Albans," the officer said, handing their passports back with a grin.

"I guess we'll have to eat in St. Albans," Sandy said to Mort as he shifted the Jag into gear. "Otherwise, we've just lied to U.S. Customs and Immigration."

On one side of the road were tall cornfields, lush, sloping hills populated with grazing cows, grain-filled silos, and ramshackle wooden barns on the verge of collapse. On the other side, the road followed the shoreline of historic Lake Champlain. Mort had seriously considered turning the car around after the border. Then the swaying rhythm of the verdant landscape calmed his nerves, the Jag gently absorbed every rise and dip in the road, and rolled in and out of wide, tree-lined curves. He was enjoying the drive.

They crossed the nature reserve at Missisquoi Bay and continued through the town centre of Swanton. On the outskirts of St. Albans, the drive-in's giant marquee sign announced a double feature, *Harry Potter and the Half-Blood Prince* and *G-Force*. A movie would definitely not be part of the evening's program.

Main Street was quiet for Saturday evening. Mort pulled the Jag into a vacant spot across from a park within walking distance of Manutti's.

"Why don't we go for a short stroll in the park before dinner?" Sandy said. "Build up an appetite. The fresh air will do us both good."

Mort didn't say no. He was beginning to allow himself the possibility of further enjoying Sandy's company.

"I don't care what my brother told me about you, or what he told you about me," Sandy said as they sat down on a bench next to a water fountain. "We're here, so let's make the best of it." The comment stung Mort. Sandy was prepared to *endure* him, meanwhile, her company was effortlessly bringing him pleasure. "My brother's intentions were good," she added.

They dined at Manutti's as planned. Mort ate veal scaloppini and Sandy had the linguini in clam sauce. They shared a carafe of house wine, Sandy drinking two glasses to Mort's one. Her appetite was hearty. She ate with gusto, convincing Mort to share tiramisu for dessert. Feeling sated after the meal, Mort described how anxious he'd been about their date. He admitted that nothing about Sandy had remotely matched his expectations, which was a good thing. Sandy expressed similar sentiments. "You're a real gentleman," she said, dabbing chocolate from the corners of her mouth with a napkin. "I'm glad we decided to stay for dinner."

Mort had enjoyed the evening so much that he almost forgot about dropping in at The Smiling Steer on the way home.

It was 9:00 p.m. when they pulled into the parking lot of the strip mall next to the interstate. Mort told Sandy about his investment in the restaurant and asked whether she minded if they dropped in for a few minutes. He suggested that she wait for him in the car. He'd only be gone for a few minutes. Impressed that as well as being a successful garment manufacturer Mort was also a restaurateur, she insisted on accompanying him inside. Why, Sandy wondered, had they not eaten at The Smiling Steer in the first place? Mort was about to answer that the Italian restaurant's menu was superior, which would have been the truth. Instead, he said that he didn't believe in mixing business with pleasure.

The dining room of The Smiling Steer was gloomy and empty. Tables were set with tablecloths, cutlery, water glasses, and lit candle centrepieces. But there was no activity, no maître d' greeting them at the entrance, no waitresses serving tables, or guests to serve, for that matter. Agitated, Mort showed Sandy to a table near the front door and asked if she would like a coffee. He went in search of a waitress. The computer screen behind the server's station was blank, the coffee pot was cold. Mort heard loud, wet, thumping coming from the kitchen. He peeked his head through the springy metal doors. The chef, dressed in a blood-spattered apron, was standing at a butcher's block, tenderizing hunks of red meat with thwacks of a blunt hammer.

"Where is everyone?" Mort yelled.

"Layoffs," was the chef's answer.

Mort would get to the bottom of this. He marched past the men's and ladies' toilets, straight to the back of the building, halting outside the manager's office. Noises could be heard through the door, the muffled sound of discussion. Mort debated whether to knock. Then he realized that the sound was only one voice not two, and it was more like moaning than talking. He turned the door handle slowly. It was unlocked. He gently pushed, letting the weight of the door carry itself open, and remained immobile in the doorway as the whine of the hinges announced his presence.

Stan Ginch sat on top of his desk, papers scattered all over the place. His trousers were dropped, bunched around his ankles. His eyes were sealed. Kneeling on the floor with his head buried between Ginch's spread hairy thighs was Manfred Goslin. For a moment it looked like worship, Goslin *shokel*ing his head back and forth in the manner of orthodox Jewish prayer in and out of his employer's lap. The boss hadn't heard the door creak open, but the employee had. Goslin stopped what he was doing, turned around and looked up at Mort. Wiping the sticky slobber from his mouth with his sleeve, he smiled a repugnant, familiar smile. Stan Ginch didn't move a muscle. He was savouring the residue of pleasure.

thirteen

Weeks later, Mort remembered his date with Sandy as another borderline fiasco in a long line of fiascos. He never said a word to her about the scene he'd witnessed in Stan Ginch's office. It would have been too humiliating. Not to say she hadn't handled the situation well, because she had — with grace and sensitivity. She didn't protest when Mort dragged her by the arm out of The Smiling Steer in a hurry. And she gave Mort his space in the car. Speeding back to the city, as the pinprick flickering of Montreal's downtown lights appeared in the dark distance, she finally spoke up, asked if everything was okay. He repeated, rather cryptically, "Never mix business and pleasure." She said nothing in response.

When they arrived at Sandy's house she got out of the Jag on her own and peeked back inside the car with a smile to thank Mort for a lovely evening. At that moment he decided that were he to bring a guest to Jackie's wedding, Sandy would definitely be his choice.

But Mort didn't invite Sandy to the wedding as his guest. He couldn't. Not because he was ashamed of it being a gay ceremony, and not because he'd been suckered by her brother into their date. Though Mort didn't relish the idea that Gerstein would get satisfaction in knowing that he had actually enjoyed Sandy's company. Let the *meshuganner* find his redemption in the Jewish afterlife by hooking up some other couple. On the contrary, as an affront to Gerstein's religious sensibilities, Mort had given thought to the notion that attending his gay son's wedding ceremony with Sandy on his arm would be a most delicious form of revenge. None of these thoughts were decisive in Mort's decision not to invite Sandy as his guest. It simply would have been in bad taste, an insult to Mona's memory, especially after Gordon's request.

"Thank you for sending all those meals. Mind the mess," Gordon said, inviting Mort into the apartment. "We still haven't finished cleaning up."

Mort had waited until the day after the *shiva* to offer Gordon his condolences. He didn't visit the house of mourning personally, but paid to send catered kosher dinners for all seven days. Mort stayed home, drank, and checked in by cellphone with Rusty and Jackie to find out how they were holding up amidst the nightly hubbub of family and visitors. It was touch and go if Rusty would *sit* with her brother and Gordon, who wasn't "officially" a mourner since he and Mona hadn't married. In the end Rusty did, with her Rav's permission, and made sure that in every possible way, the period of mourning would respect Jewish law and tradition, even if the home where they sat wasn't kosher. Mendel Fuchs led prayer services morning and evening, and made certain that they would never be a man short for a *minyan*.

Mona's death was a shock. It had hit Mort much harder than he'd ever expected it would. Diagnosed only weeks before calling Mort to tell him about Jackie's wedding plans, she'd kept her illness a secret. Rusty had briefly become suspicious when her mother began requesting to borrow books on Jewish spirituality.

Mona explained that wedding preparations had inspired her newfound interest. The cancer spread quickly. She hadn't completed her first full round of chemo before she was admitted to the hospital with severe palpitations.

Hearing the news that Mona was in the hospital, Mort began piecing together certain memories: the head scarf she'd worn at the El Morocco; Gordon entering the Jewish General Hospital; Mona speaking about God on the phone. She lasted less than forty-eight hours.

Gordon told Mort that he felt as if he'd been run over by an eighteen-wheeler. "We thought she was being admitted to treat an arrhythmia of the heart. They were going to adjust her meds. She was doing relatively well up to that point. It happened literally overnight. She went into cardiac arrest. We had no idea that she wouldn't be coming out."

"What are you going to do now?" Mort asked.

"Well, clean up, for one thing. There's a lot to take care of, papers to put in order, that sort of thing," Gordon sighed. Then the fatigue faded from Gordon's eyes as he looked at Mort.

"Mona made a request. Something important. Of course, it wasn't part of the plan that she wouldn't live long enough to see Jacob get married. You know how much that meant to her. She worked so hard to arrange the room, the flowers, the music, the meal. She was always so skilled at making arrangements. Of course, she was acting with a sense of urgency. Near the end she asked me to ask you something. I know how you feel about the marriage. Now that she's gone, perhaps you'll reconsider. Mona's request requires your involvement Mort —"

The three-piece ensemble, clarinet, keyboard, and stand-up bass played "My Boy" instead of "The Wedding March." It was Jackie's tribute to his father. The rest was more or less traditional. The rabbi stood under a *chuppah* at the end of a long, red-carpeted centre aisle, rows of invited guests seated on either side. The wedding canopy was white with long vines of red and green heart-shaped leaves twined concentrically up the four *chuppah* posts.

The search for a rabbi had turned up a ringer, a clergyman who had all his bases covered, religiously speaking. He was a free agent (without a congregation), raised Orthodox in Montreal, ordained Reconstructionist in Philadelphia, and was licensed in both Quebec and Ontario, where he occasionally pinch-hit for a reform congregation in Ottawa. He'd answered the newspaper ad in *The Globe and Mail*: "Montreal gay couple seeking rabbi to perform traditional-type nuptials. Only strictly observant clergy need apply." Jackie and Noah said they loved him from their very first phone conversation.

Rabbi Weinstock was friendly and open to suggestions, though, not so open as to easily dispense with ancient practice. He agreed with the boys that they could partake in most of the age-old Jewish marriage rituals, although several would need to be altered to suit the occasion. The *ketubah*, for example, was somewhat problematic. The traditional marriage contract contained certain phrases that were not appropriate. Fortunately, the boys found an online Judaica dealer who specialized in *ketubot* that were tailored for a variety of permutations and combinations. She offered a wide-ranging collection of exquisite marriage contracts that covered the spectrum of Jewish tradition, from Sephardic and Ashkenazi, to Orthodox and Conservative, to Reconstructionist, Reform, and Jewish Renewal. The documents were elegantly scripted in calligraphy on parchment in a host of colours and designs, from Jerusalemite to contemporary geometric to Asian floral. There were certificates for gay and lesbian marriages, mixed marriages, also Messianic Jewish marriages (a.k.a. Jews for Jesus), atheist, agnostic, and even "non-committal" marriages.

Other marriage traditions needed tweaking to fit Jackie and Noah's matrimonial needs or would have to be replaced altogether. For the *bedekin* prior to the signing of the *ketubah*, in which the Jewish bride was ceremoniously veiled by the groom, the boys would each "bedeck" the other in his *tallit* and matching navy velveteen *kippah*. Also, wedding vows would be rewritten by Jackie and Noah to include their heartfelt personal sentiments. The *Sheva Berachot*, the Seven Blessings, would be said without alteration. Rings would be exchanged, and after the vows were uttered, there would be two glasses, one for each partner, shattered in unison, symbolizing the destruction of the First and Second Jerusalem Temples.

"I had nothing to do with it," Mort answered Officer Potente who was sitting on the couch across from him, not looking nearly as comfortable as he did the last time he visited.

"I know that you did. But since the investigation is closed and the fire was officially ruled accidental, an act of God, there's really nothing more for me to do. The sale of the house will go through and the insurance will pay out." Potente paused thoughtfully. "I must say, your request to go to Saint Leonard came out of left field. I thought you were cracking. Then I thought to myself that it wasn't such a bad idea. Seeing all those places where there were fires. It might help to jog your memory. Firebugs are obsessive. Everything about fires excites them, even just being in proximity to past fires. And there are plenty of those in Saint Leo."

"I'm not a firebug."

"No. I suppose not. I don't know how you did it, or who you hired to do it. But it was professional. I figure that if you hired someone, you told them what to do. No one knew that house better than you did, inside and out, every stone, every plank, and every strand of brittle wire. Since you're immune from prosecution, why not 'fess up, as one professional to another?"

"I don't know what you're talking about."

"I didn't think so. Well, it was worth a try." Potente held up the box. "Here. Consider this a token of my admiration." When he saw a gift-wrapped box, Mort had thought that Potente had come to deliver a wedding gift for Jackie. The arson investigator leaned forward and placed the gift next to Mort on top of his drink stand. "You can open it after I leave," he said, standing up.

Mort poured himself a celebratory glass of Crown Royal before tearing open the box. The polished silver jaguar lay on her side in a bed of black felt. She was magnificent, a timeless treasure, like an Egyptian artifact in a tiny sarcophagus, asleep and dreaming for three thousand years. A gulp of liquor burned down Mort's throat and spread inside his chest like a flame.

There were times in his life when Mort neglected to act and regretted it later. And there were other times when he took decisive action without being exactly sure why. Action had not always required a long period of gestation. Mort's instruction to his Miami attorney, Gaylon Samberg, was direct and without much forethought. "No one must know," he said.

Gaylon had handled the purchase of his beachfront apartment in Sunrise, and he was the secretary of Mort's Bahamian corporation. As with the Florida apartment transaction, the attorney dutifully followed Mort's instructions without asking questions. The unsolicited offer on 92 Hampstead Road had to be high enough to guarantee acceptance without the delays and messiness of back-and-forth negotiations.

The offer was made by Gaylon, acting on behalf of the Bahamian corporation and delivered through the law offices of Markus, Gitelman, and Sauvé in Montreal, a firm with whom Gaylon had done business in the past. Mort's regular lawyer, Mel Grand, knew nothing about it. Mort wanted to be sure that the purchase had no discernible connection to him. This manoeuvre would represent the repatriation of a solid chunk of the money he'd been stashing offshore for years. It was risky business.

Did he ever think that an underlying vindictiveness against Mona was at the heart of his decision to buy 92 from the Shines? Mort had harboured a certain amount of resentment. Letting her have the house in the divorce settlement made sense for two reasons. First, it would minimize the upheaval in their kids' lives. They would maintain a semblance of family home life with their mother until they were old enough to move out on their own.

Second, it was a necessary move, financially. Mona held a trump card. She knew everything about the offshore accounts and could spill the beans to the authorities at any time. He was already on their radar screen because of BestTex. Ninety-two Hampstead Road was Mort's concession, payment for Mona's indefinite silence. When she sold the house to the Shines, he felt blindsided. She never consulted him, not even as a courtesy. They had, or so he thought, an unspoken understanding that he had a claim on the house. He vowed that one day he would get the house back, somehow, or at least make sure that if he couldn't own it, no one else ever would.

The visits to 92 after the fire had slowly torn Mort apart. *Our lives are vestiges that we cling to*, he told himself. Everything ends in rubble and dust. The house had to be sacrificed. The preservation of a person's dignity, sanity, and memory comes at a price. "Make sure that the Shines are carrying sufficient insurance," Mort had ordered Gaylon. "Then find a way to get the job done."

Mort was not emotionally prepared to witness his former home in ruins; the bulldozers excavating the rooms, the piles of charred debris. His memories flowed and it took time, but eventually he felt that the flames could purify him and his dignity could be reconstructed out of ash and rubble. And through it all the stone had remained fortifying him emotionally.

When the walls were torn down, too, and all that was left of 92 Hampstead Road was a vacant lot, Mort felt personally exposed in a way he could not have anticipated. He was plunged into despair. It was at that point when clarity came to him. He might have been the one who built the house. He might have always imagined it to be his personal domain, his accomplishment, a monument to his aspiration and industriousness. But it was never really his. Everything he'd done was for his children. He'd built a house, but Jackie and Rusty made it a home. It belonged to them.

Mort wrote two notes. Both said exactly the same words:

> *Dear Jackie and Rusty,*
> *Don't think of the enclosed cheque as a gift (except for tax purposes). The money comes from the home where you grew up that no longer exists. Spend it as you wish. The cheque comes with a vacant lot in Hampstead. The land is my gift to you. It signifies the possibility of fresh beginnings, new life. No strings attached. You can build two new houses where our home once stood (the lot is big enough). Or you can spend the money some other way and sell the land. It's up to you.*

At the bottom of Jackie's note Mort added, *Mazel tov on your wedding. You've made me very proud!*

Rabbi Weinstock waited under the centre of the wedding canopy. At either corner behind him, two video spotlights bright as car headlights shone blindingly down the aisle, making the figure of the rabbi appear to the members of the procession like a faceless shadow.

Jackie and Noah had considered the order of the traditional procession carefully and decided that it was objectionable. The practice of the groom walking down the aisle first and waiting for his bride to be handed over implied subservience and inequality, like she was bought property being delivered by a vendor to a purchaser. They agreed that they would walk down the aisle unescorted as a statement of personal empowerment and individuality. The question of how the parents would be included in the procession was answered by Mona. After speaking with Gordon, Mort agreed to honour her wishes. He preceded his son down the aisle with Gordon, arm in arm. They walked slowly, which suited Mort. They smiled to family and friends, who smiled and stared back, some delighted, others in disbelief. A severely scaled-down delegation of the Snowdon Deli gang sat together about halfway down the aisle: Hershey Blank and his wife next to Bookie Moss and his girlfriend. They nodded at Mort and he nodded back. Mort stumbled on a carpet wrinkle near the front row. Gordon caught him firmly by the elbow. The misstep was hardly noticed by anyone.

If there was a credo that Mort had tried to live by — though, he never thought in such terms — it would go something like this: *do what you want to do*. A person had to cheat life, dodge its potholes, and steer clear of its many hazards. Whether or not you did what you *wanted* to do in life was the measure of a man. It was simply the only sure way to avoid disappointment. Mort admitted that he'd not been completely successful at always doing what he wanted to do. His disappointments loomed large. Mona was right about that. These were his thoughts while he stood next to his son under the *chuppah*, listening to the rabbi recite the blessing over the cup of wine to signify a moment of importance and celebration. He shook his head and smiled. By his own standards, Jackie was a winner. He was doing exactly what he *wanted* to do and was getting away with it. To Mort, this gay wedding now seemed like one of the all-time great feats; not just a home run, but a goddamn third-decker, grand-slam homerun.

Better still, it was akin to the most daring play of all in baseball. A play so brazen, so dazzling, and rare that every baseball fan considers himself lucky to witness it in person a few times in his life: it was like stealing home. And instantly, under the *chuppah* standing between Gordon and his son, listening to the rabbi chant, Mort's mind shifted back to another place and another time, to Wednesday, September 28, 1955, Game 1 of the World Series, another New York Yankees — Brooklyn Dodgers match-up. It was not a game Mort had attended, but he remembered it like it was yesterday and guarded the memory close to his heart, for two reasons. First, 1955 would be the only World Championship victory of Jackie Robinson's legendary nine-year Major League baseball career, and the only championship won by the Dodgers while they were still in Brooklyn. After two more seasons playing in Brooklyn the team would be shipped off to become the Los Angeles Dodgers that, decades later, would go on to defeat the Montreal Expos on Blue Monday.

The second reason Game 1 of the 1955 series was on Mort's mind was that Jackie Robinson accomplished the unthinkable. With two outs in the eighth inning and the Dodgers trailing 6–4, Robinson took a long lead off third base, got a huge jump on the wind-up of Yankee pitching ace Whitey Ford, and slid cleats-first underneath the mitt of catcher Yogi Berra blocking the plate. He was called safe by the umpire: Jackie Robinson stole home.

From one Jackie to another. Mort's Jackie was playing the game his own way, breaking barriers, and beating the odds. Mort's Jackie was as daring and dazzling as his namesake. He felt proud of his son.

The only question lingering in Mort's mind now was whether he would be able to stomach watching husband and husband kiss. He patted his tuxedo jacket nervously to feel for the presence of the cheque-filled envelope he'd give Jackie when the ceremony was over. He'd left Rusty's envelope at home.

acknowledgements

I am grateful to the following people who took the time to help: Arleen Solomon Rotchin, Randy Rotchin, Annetta Black, Jamie Malus, Mark Smilovitch, David Bornstein, Milly Marmur, David Hamburg, and Beverley Slopen.

Special thanks to Carolyn Forde for keeping the faith, Shannon Whibbs for her editorial expertise, Claudio Bisinella for introducing me to *his* Saint-Leo, and especially to my father, Ezra Rotchin, for sharing his stories.

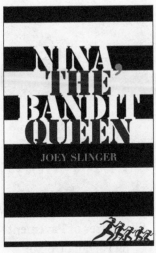

Nina, the Bandit Queen
by Joey Slinger
978-1459701380
$21.99

In a part of town so beaten down that even prostitutes and drug dealers have written if off, Nina Dolgoy imagines that if the local pool wasn't boarded up, her little daughters could burn their wayward energy off in it and avoid falling into utter degradation. So she leads her neighbours on a fundraising, pool-fixing community-improvement campaign. Given her skill set, however, the only way Nina can think to raise money herself is by robbing a bank. Unfortunately, she isn't very good at it. This is only the start of Nina's problems, which grow until they culminate in a sublimely bizarre chase during which Nina somehow needs to pull the wool over everybody's eyes.

Six Metres of Pavement
by Farzana Doctor
978-1554887675
$22.99

Ismail Boxwala made the worst mistake of his life one morning
twenty years ago: he forgot his baby daughter in the back seat of
his car. After her tragic death, he struggles to continue living. A
divorce, years of heavy drinking, and sex with strangers only leave
him more alone and isolated. But Ismail's story begins to change
after he reluctantly befriends two women: Fatima, a young queer
activist kicked out of her parents' home; and Celia, his grieving
Portuguese-Canadian neighbour who lives just six metres away.
A slow-simmering romance develops between Ismail and Celia.
Meanwhile, dangers lead Fatima to his doorstep. Each makes
complicated demands of him, ones he is uncertain he can meet.

Waiting for Ricky Tantrum
by Jules Lewis
978-1554887408
$17.99

Jim Myers is a painfully shy kid living in Toronto's west end Bloorcourt Village. After school he hangs around with his neighbour and only friend, Oleg Khernofsky, playing basketball against a NO PARKING sign in a laneway. In the evenings, he haunts Nicky's Diner. On the first day of junior high, Jim crosses paths with Charlie Crouse, a brash, mouthy kid full of wild stories about his past. Charlie takes Jim under his wing and introduces him to the electronic strip poker machine at the Fun Village Arcade in Koreatown, a Queen Street hooker who calls herself Steffi Graf, and the diverse sounds and utterances of his landlord's three lovers. As Jim and Charlie's friendship grows, however, the realities of looming adulthood seep into their lives with surprising consequences.

DUNDURN
www.dundurn.com

What did you think of this book?
Visit www.dundurn.com for reviews, videos, updates, and more!